Step into the world of NYC Angels

Looking out over Central Park,
the Angel Mendez Children's Hospital,
affectionately known as Angel's,
is famed throughout America for being at the
forefront of paediatric medicine, with talented
staff who always go that extra mile for their
little patients. Their lives are full of highs,
lows, drama and emotion.

In the city that never sleeps, the life-saving
docs at Angel's Hospital work hard, play hard
and love even harder. There's *always* time
for some sizzling after-hours romance…

And striding the halls of the hospital,
leaving a sea of fluttering hearts behind him,
is the dangerously charismatic new head of
neurosurgery Alejandro Rodriguez. But there's
one woman, paediatrician Layla Woods, who's
left an indelible mark on his no-go-area heart.
Expect their reunion to be explosive!

NYC Angels

*Children's doctors who work hard and love
even harder…in the city that never sleeps!*

Dear Reader

I am thrilled to have been asked to provide Book Six for this eight-book continuity about Angel Mendez Children's Hospital, set in New York City, just a few hours from my home. It was an honour to work with the wonderfully talented authors who contributed to this series.

My story is about Scarlet, the head nurse of the hospital's NICU—Neonatal Intensive Care Unit—and Lewis, the head of the hospital's paediatric emergency room.

Since I have no first-hand knowledge of NICUs, this book took quite a bit of research to pull off. But I love learning new things, and now have a healthy respect for the hard-working nurses and doctors who provide care to the tiniest of patients and their families.

In this story I touch on the issue of adoption, a topic near and dear to my heart as I was adopted. It takes a special person willing to make a lifetime commitment to adopting, taking care of and loving another person's child from birth through adulthood, or any-where in between. I hope I did the storyline justice.

I love to hear from readers! Please contact me at Wendy@WendySMarcus.com

Thank you for buying and reading my books.

Wishing you all good things

Wendy S. Marcus

NYC ANGELS: TEMPTING NURSE SCARLET

BY
WENDY S. MARCUS

This book is dedicated to men and women around the world
who have found room in their hearts to love and nurture someone else's
child and in the process make them their own—like my parents did.
With special thanks to my wonderfully supportive editor, Flo Nicoll.
I don't know how I'd make it from the beginning to The End without
your guidance and encouragement. You are an absolute gem!
And to my loving family for making me food, for making me laugh,
and for making me proud. And, in case you're wondering,
yes, my husband does read my books!

First published in Great Britain 2013
by Mills & Boon, an imprint of Harlequin (UK) Limited,
Large Print edition 2013
Harlequin (UK) Limited, Eton House,
18-24 Paradise Road, Richmond, Surrey TW9 1SR

© Harlequin Books S.A. 2013

Special thanks and acknowledgement are given
to Wendy S. Marcus for her contribution to the
NYC Angels series

ISBN: 978 0 263 23140 3

Harlequin (UK) policy is to use papers that are natural, renewable and recyclable products and made from wood grown in sustainable forests. The logging and manufacturing process conform to the legal environmental regulations of the country of origin.

Printed and bound in Great Britain
by CPI Antony Rowe, Chippenham, Wiltshire

Wendy S. Marcus is not a lifelong reader. As a child she never burrowed under her covers with a flashlight and a good book. In senior English she skimmed the classics, reading the bare minimum required to pass the class. Wendy found her love of reading later in life, in a box of old paperbacks at a school fundraiser where she was introduced to the romance genre in the form of a Harlequin Superromance. Since that first book she's been a voracious reader of romance—oftentimes staying up way too late in order to reach the happy ending before letting herself go to sleep.

Wendy lives in the beautiful Hudson Valley region of New York, with her husband, two of their three children, and their beloved dog Buddy. A nurse by trade, Wendy has a Master's degree in healthcare administration. After years of working in the medical profession she's taken a radical turn to write hot, contemporary romances with strong heroes, feisty heroines and lots of laughs. Wendy loves hearing from readers. Please visit her blog at www.WendySMarcus.com

Recent titles by the same author:

SECRETS OF A SHY SOCIALITE*
CRAVING HER SOLDIER'S TOUCH*
THE NURSE'S NOT-SO-SECRET SCANDAL
ONCE A GOOD GIRL…
WHEN ONE NIGHT ISN'T ENOUGH

*Beyond the Spotlight

**These books are also available
in eBook format from www.millsandboon.co.uk**

NYC Angels

Children's doctors who work hard and love even harder…
in the city that never sleeps!
Step into the world of NYC Angels
and enjoy two new stories a month

New York's most notoriously sinful bachelor Jack Carter
finds a woman he wants to spend more than just one night with in:
NYC ANGELS: REDEEMING THE PLAYBOY
by Carol Marinelli

And reluctant socialite Eleanor Aston makes the gossip headlines
when the paparazzi discover her baby bombshell:
NYC ANGELS: HEIRESS'S BABY SCANDAL
by Janice Lynn

Cheery physiotherapist Molly Shriver melts the icy barricades
around hotshot surgeon Dan Morris's damaged heart in:
NYC ANGELS: UNMASKING DR SERIOUS
by Laura Iding

And Lucy Edwards is finally tempted to let neurosurgeon
Ryan O'Doherty in. But their fragile relationship will need
to survive her most difficult revelation yet…
NYC ANGELS: THE WALLFLOWER'S SECRET
by Susan Carlisle

Newly single (and strictly off-limits!)
Chloe Jenkins makes it very difficult for drop-dead-gorgeous
Brad Davis to resist temptation…!
NYC ANGELS: FLIRTING WITH DANGER
by Tina Beckett

And after meeting single dad Lewis Jackson, tough-cookie
Head Nurse Scarlet Miller wonders if she's finally met her match…
NYC ANGELS: TEMPTING NURSE SCARLET
by Wendy S. Marcus

Bubbly new nurse Polly Seymour
is the ray of sunshine brooding doc Johnny Griffin needs in:
NYC ANGELS: MAKING THE SURGEON SMILE
by Lynne Marshall

And Alex Rodriguez and Layla Woods come back into each other's
orbit, trying to fool the buzzing hospital grapevine that the spark
between them has died. But can they convince each other?
NYC ANGELS: AN EXPLOSIVE REUNION
by Alison Roberts

Be captivated by NYC Angels in this new eight-book continuity
from Mills & Boon® Medical Romance™

These books are also available in eBook format
from www.millsandboon.co.uk

CHAPTER ONE

SCARLET MILLER, head nurse of the NICU—Neonatal Intensive Care Unit—at Angel Mendez Children's Hospital, lovingly referred to as Angel's by the staff, walked onto the brand new, now fully functioning unit she'd played a key role in designing and creating, feeling more at home than she did anywhere else. Feeling proud of all she and her wonderful colleagues had accomplished, during her four years as a manager—national recognition for providing the highest level of care available for sick and premature newborns with one of the lowest mortality rates in the U.S. A high tech yet caring, state of the art yet warm and welcoming sixty-two bed unit that the residents of New York City and its surrounding areas kept at or near full capacity on a regular basis.

"Looks like someone finally had herself a hot

weekend," Linda, one of her older nurses said, walking up beside her. At least she wasn't complaining about the switch from the open floor plan of their old setup to the mostly private rooms of their new wing.

"If by someone you're referring to me." Scarlet stopped at the nurses' station, took the pink message slips held up by one of the unit secretaries and gave the young woman a smile of thanks before turning back to Linda. "And if by hot you're referring to my oppressive, sweat-drenched, Saturday night of misery, the hottest eleventh day of May ever recorded in Weehawken, New Jersey, during which I spent more than sixteen hours without power ergo without air conditioning, then yes. I did indeed have a hot weekend."

"Uh oh." Linda glanced toward a huge vase filled with at least two dozen long-stemmed red roses and accenting ferns perched on the counter to their left.

"Uh oh what?" Scarlet asked.

"I told you we shouldn't do it," Ashley, the young secretary said, shaking her head.

Scarlet looked at her. "Do what?"

Cindy, one of her newest nurses, who'd been observing patient monitors and video feeds as part of her orientation, looked up over the counter and pointed to a rectangular golden box of chocolates, the cover askew.

"Would someone please tell me what's going on?" Scarlet didn't have time to play around, she needed to get back to work after a morning of meetings and greet the family of their newest micro-preemie, baby girl Gupta, born at twenty-six weeks, one pound, thirteen ounces, thirteen inches long, who'd arrived during her absence.

"We thought they were yours," Cindy said.

"What—?"

"The flowers. And the chocolates," she clarified.

"Why…" would they think someone had sent her red roses, the floral symbol of love and passion, typically given by men to their wives, girlfriends, and lovers, when she practically lived at the hospital, and hadn't had a man in her life since… Hmmm. Since…

She gave up rather than belabor the pitiful fact it'd been so long she'd require a quick browse of her calendar, from last year, or Lord help her, maybe the year before, to spark her memory. Not that she'd humiliate herself by actually looking. But in her defense, no woman could have achieved the level of success she'd managed—which benefited the hospital, its tiniest patients and their families as much as it did her—without putting in long hours on the job.

"Because the card that accompanied them is made out to you." Linda pointed to the mini mint green envelope sticking out of the beautiful, fragrant, partially opened blooms which did in fact have her name on it. Spelled with one t unlike the famous Scarlett she'd been named after—only her mother hadn't taken the time to get the spelling right.

Scarlet plucked the card from its plastic holder and opened it.

Dear Scarlet,
I realize you never told me your last name.
I hope these get to you. Saturday night was
better than I'd ever imagined a night with a
woman could be.

Right there Scarlet knew the card wasn't meant for her. But she read on…not to snoop, mind you, but to search out any identifying information on the intended recipient.

Let's do it again soon.
Good luck at your new job.
Call me,
Brandon

Beneath his name he'd listed his home telephone number, his work number, cell number, and e-mail address. Scarlet's namesake must be pretty darn good in the sack. "Call down to Human Resources," she told Ashley. "Ask if there's a new hire named Scarlet and where she works."

While Ashley did as instructed, Cindy grabbed the card from Scarlet's hand and read it. "Yowza." She used the card to fan herself then handed it to Linda.

"Mercy me," Linda said. "You girls today." She shook her head in disapproval.

Ashley put down the phone and looked up apologetically. "A Scarlett, with two 't's, Ryan began work as a unit secretary in the pediatric ER today."

"And you all," Scarlet pointed to each of the chocolate eating culprits while squinting her eyes in playful accusation, "ate the poor girl's hard-earned chocolates."

"We had help," Linda said. "It's an unwritten rule that chocolates at a nursing station are fair game. Dig in or don't complain when you miss out. No invitation needed."

"Nursing is a stressful occupation," Cindy added. "Nurses need chocolate to help us cope and keep us happy so we can be at our caring and competent best." She snapped her fingers. "If you give me a few minutes I bet I can find a research study to support that."

Scarlet smiled. "What's the damage?" She lifted the lid. One lone milk chocolate remained in the upper right corner surrounded by approximately thirty empty little square partitions. And it'd been squeezed to reveal its dark pink center.

"I told them to save you one," Ashley said.

"We think it's raspberry," Cindy added.

"You like raspberry," Linda chimed in.

Since it wasn't in good enough shape to offer up as an 'at least I managed to save you one' peace offering, Scarlet popped the partially mutilated chocolate into her mouth. Yup. Raspberry. Surrounded by creamy, rich, delicious chocolate. She held off swallowing to draw out the experience. Then fought the urge to inhale and let her eyes drift closed to savor the pleasure. Pathetic. "Back to work. All of you," she said with a few shoos of her hands.

"What are you going to do about the chocolates?" Ashley asked.

You. Not we. Because Scarlet always stood up for her staff. No matter what. She replaced the cover and flung the box into the garbage can. "What chocolates?" she asked with an innocent smile.

Her staff smiled back.

"What about the flowers?" Ashley asked.

Scarlet carefully placed the card back in the envelope, tucked in the flap, and inserted it back into its plastic pronged holder. "I'll bring them down to the ER after I check in on little Miss Gupta."

As far as bad days went—and Dr. Lewis Jackson, head of the Pediatric Emergency Room at Angel's, had experienced some pretty hellacious ones over the past nine months, since finding out he was the father and new primary caregiver to his demon of a now thirteen-year-old daughter—today was shaping up to be one of the worst.

Two nurses out sick. A new unit secretary, who, while nice to look at, had clearly overstated her abilities, and Jessie, taken into police custody for shoplifting at a drug store and truancy.

The one bright spot in his afternoon, whether because of his scrubs and hospital ID, or Angel's excellent reputation, or Jessie's difficult past year, the police officer in charge had convinced the store manager to let her off with a warning.

Lewis stood on the curb outside the police station and raised his arm up high to hail a cab. "This is by far the stupidest and most inconsiderate stunt you've pulled since you've gotten here." And that was saying something. A yellow minivan taxi pulled to a stop. Lewis slid open the rear door, grabbed Jessie by her arms and pushed her in ahead of him.

"Angel Mendez Children's Hospital," he told the driver then closed the door. "Pediatric Emergency Room entrance. And if you can get us there in under fifteen minutes I'll give you an extra twenty."

At the added incentive, the driver swerved back into traffic, cutting off another taxi. And a bus. And almost taking out a bike-riding delivery man. Horns honked. Drivers yelled out their open windows. Middle fingers flew. A typical taxi ride in New York City.

Lewis turned his attention back to Jessie. "What were you thinking?" Leaving school. Wandering the streets of Manhattan. Unaccompanied. Unsupervised. Unprotected. At the thought of all the terrible things that could have happened to her fear knotted his gut.

Per usual Jessie didn't look at him. She just sat there in her baggy black clothes, mad at the world, and ignored him. But this time when she reached into her pocket for the beloved ear buds she used to effectively drown him out with vile music, which would likely be responsible for permanent damage to her eardrums, he yanked the white cords from her hands. "I'm talking to you, young lady. And this time you are going to listen."

She glared at him in response.

"Your behavior is unacceptable, and I have had enough. I'm sorry your mother passed away. I'm sorry she never told me about you." And even sorrier she'd spent so much of her time bad-mouthing him to the point Jessie had hated him at first sight without ever giving him a chance. "I'm sorry your life was uprooted from Maryland to the heart of New York City. I'm sorry I work such long hours. But I'm all you have. And I'm trying."

He'd given up his privacy, his freedom, and a very active and satisfying sex life to spend quality time with and be a good role model for his daughter. He'd hired nannies to watch her after school when he had to work, while she'd achieved new heights of belligerent teenage obnoxiousness to the point none stayed longer than a month. He'd hired a car service to take her to and from school on days he couldn't, while she didn't show up to meet them at the designated times and locations, leaving them to wait, and charge him for every minute. He brought home pizza, thinking all kids loved pizza. Jessie wanted Chinese food. He brought home Chinese food, she wanted Italian. He'd gotten her a fancy cellphone so they could keep in touch while he was working. To date, she hadn't responded to one of his calls or text messages. And the only time she'd used it to contact him was today, to ask him to come down to the police station.

He was trying, dammit. Was it too much to expect her to try, too?

"You left me at that police station for two hours." Her words oozed accusation and anger.

"Because I was at work when you pulled your little caper, and I don't have the type of job where I can run out at a moment's notice. I have a responsibility to my patients. I had to call in another doctor, on his day off, pay him overtime, and wait for him to come in and cover for me before I could leave."

Jessie crossed her arms over her chest and said, "I hate you."

No surprise there. "Well I've got news for you." Lewis crossed his arms over his chest, just like his stubborn, moody daughter, and glared right back at her. "Right now I hate you, too."

The second the words left his mouth he hated himself more. Lewis Jackson, the over-achiever who never failed at anything was failing at single parenthood. Even worse, he was failing his troubled young daughter.

The taxi screeched to a halt at their destination with one minute to spare. Jessie was out of the cab and heading to the electric doors before Lewis had even paid. After practically throwing the fare, plus tip and a crisp twenty dollar bill, at the driver, he slid out and ran to catch up. "Jessie. Wait."

She didn't.

He ran into the ER. "Don't you dare—"

Jessie broke into a run, heading toward the back hallway.

Lewis took off after her. Not again. He rounded the corner in time to see the door to the unisex disabled bathroom slam shut. He reached it just in time to hear the lock click into place. Again. He banged on the door. "Dammit, Jessie, get out here." So he could apologize. So he could try to make her understand. So he could drag her into his office and barricade her inside so, for the next few hours at least, he'd know she was safe.

He paced. Flexed and extended his fingers. Felt wound too tight. And realized maybe it was best she didn't come out. Because she had him vacillating between wanting to hit her and wanting to hug her, between yelling at her and throwing himself to the ground at her feet and begging her for mercy, between letting her continue to stay with him and researching strict European boarding schools that allow only supervised visitation—once a year.

Never in his adult life had he felt this indecisive and ineffective and totally, overwhelmingly, embarrassingly inept.

"Jessie," he said through the door, trying the knob just in case. Locked. "Please come out."

He used his calm voice. "I need to get back to work." And he didn't want to leave her when she was so upset.

When *he* was so upset.

She didn't respond which didn't come as a surprise since she hadn't responded to any of the other dozen/thirty/hundred times he'd called to her through a locked door. He pictured her smiling on the other side deriving some perverse sense of satisfaction from him standing in the hallway, frustrated, enraged, and in danger of losing what little control he had left.

Well enough of that.

"Fine." He stormed back to the nurses' station. "Call Maintenance," he snapped at the new unit secretary who seemed to be paying more attention to a huge glass vase filled with roses than doing her job.

He waited for her to return to her phone where she belonged.

"Tell them I need the door to the bathroom in

the rear corridor opened again. And this time I want them to bring me a copy of the key."

As soon as she confirmed someone would be up in a few minutes, he hurried back to the bathroom, hoping Jessie hadn't taken the opportunity of his absence to escape and disappear until it was time to go home.

After the initial shock of finding out he was the father of a pre-teen girl, Lewis had actually gotten kind of excited at the prospect of sharing the city he loved with his daughter, taking her on bike rides in Central Park and to museums and shows, the ballet and opera, of immersing her in culture and introducing her to new experiences, teaching and nurturing her, and guiding her into adulthood.

At least until he'd met her.

Lewis rounded the corner and stopped short at the sight of Jessie standing in the hallway, facing away from him, talking to a brown-haired female hospital employee he didn't recognize. But she wore light blue hospital scrubs covered by a short white lab coat typically worn by staff in management or supervisory positions.

"Now he won't make me go to stupid Lake George," Jessie said. "I'm too bad. His parents won't be able to handle me."

Rage like he'd never before experienced forced him forward. "That's why you broke the law?" he bellowed as he stormed toward Jessie. "That's why you risked getting arrested and going in front of a judge and having to do hours of community service or some other punishment? To get out of a fun Memorial Day weekend trip with your grandparents and cousins? Of all the stupid—"

Jessie crossed her arms, locked her left leg, and jutted out her left hip, taking on her defiant pose. "I told you I don't want to go."

"Well I've got news for you, young lady. My mind is made up and my decision is final. You *are* going to Lake George." In eleven days. Because Lewis needed a break and sex and a few days to re-visit his old, relaxed, likable self, to clear his head and come up with a new approach to handling his daughter, calmly and rationally.

"He wants to get rid of me." Jessie threw herself at the stranger who barely managed to get her arms up in time to catch her.

Not permanently. Just for a brief respite. "I—"

"He doesn't want me," she cried. "He never wanted me. My mom told me so. Now that she's gone I have no one."

Lewis's chest tightened at the devastation in her voice. No, children were not part of his life plan. But since the paternity test had proved Jessie to be his biological daughter, even though she'd gotten her pretty face and unpleasant temperament from her mother, he was determined to do the best job he could raising her. A task that'd turned out to be much more difficult than he'd ever imagined.

"Jessie—" He reached for her, wanting to be the one to hold her and comfort her.

But Jessie held up her hand as she sucked in a few choppy breaths and cried out,

"He says I have to stay there. No matter what. And I can't come home early."

"Because I have to work," Lewis lied. But it sounded better than, "Because I need some time away from you to regain my sanity."

"You work all the time," she accused, scowling at him over the stranger's shoulder.

"And why should it matter if I do?" Lewis shot back. "It's not like I can get you to go anywhere or do anything with me when I'm not working."

"See how he talks to me?" Jessie said. "He hates me."

"You're laying it on a bit thick, don't you think?" the woman asked, peeling Jessie's arms off of her and stepping away, giving Lewis his first view of her name tag. Scarlet Miller, RN, BSN, MSN, CCRN. Head Nurse NICU.

"I'm totally serious," Jessie said, wiping her eyes with the backs of her hands. "He told me so." She glared at him. "In the taxi on the way here."

Scarlet turned her assessing gaze on him.

"Wow," she said, shaking her head. "And all this time I've been telling Jessie you couldn't possibly be as big a jerk as she was making you out to be. I stand corrected."

Her keen blue eyes locked with his in challenge. Her face—an attractive mix of natural beauty and intelligence—in full view for the first time, Lewis lost track of the conversation for a few seconds, moving his focus to her chocolate brown hair and pleasingly trim figure. Her confident stance as she berated him. Her statement of "all this time" registered bringing him full circle to wonder why a professional adult female, who looked to be closer to his age than his daughter's, would befriend a little girl.

"If he makes me go I'll run away," Jessie said to Scarlet as if Lewis wasn't standing right there.

"No you won't," Scarlet said firmly.

Good. Another adult on his side.

"You did," Jessie accused.

What kind of nut job shared that information with a confused little girl?

"Did you not listen when I told you what a dangerous and stupid move it was?" She took Jessie by the shoulders and turned her. "Look at me, Jess."

Jess. So familiar. So caring.

The vulnerable expression on his daughter's face as she obeyed, gave him his first opportunity to see beneath her tough-teen anger and defiance to the scared little girl she'd hidden away so effectively, from him, but not this stranger. Why?

"You have what I didn't. You have me." The woman dug into the pocket of her lab coat, pulled out a business card, and wrote something on the back. Then she held it out to Jessie. "On the front is my work number and on the back is my cell phone number. You can call me anytime for any reason. I didn't offer earlier because I didn't want to interfere between you and your dad."

As it should be.

"You are not all alone, Jess. You have your father and you have me." Scarlet glanced at him before continuing. "And if, while you're on vacation, someone tries to make you do something you don't want to do or in any way makes you feel uncomfortable and your dad won't come up to bring you home, I promise I will."

Oh no she would not. "My daughter will be driven to and from Lake George by her grandparents. And she doesn't need your telephone numbers because if she needs to talk to someone anytime for any reason, she can talk to me." Lewis grabbed for the card.

Jessie thrust it behind her back.

"This entire situation is getting out of hand, Jess," Scarlet said. "You need to tell him."

Lewis stopped and looked at her. "Tell me what?"

"What's said between us stays between us," Jessie yelled at Scarlet. "You promised."

"That was before you got yourself picked up by the police and threatened to run away."

"You mean you know—?" Lewis started only to be cut off when an urgent voice came through the overhead speakers. "Scarlet Miller to the emergency room. Stat. Scarlet Miller to the emergency room."

"Saved by the hospital operator," Scarlet said with a wink to Jessie. "Talk to your father," she added before turning her back on him and walking away.

CHAPTER TWO

SCARLET JOGGED THE short distance to the large nurses' station in the center of the busy emergency room. "I'm Scarlet Miller," she said to the Scarlett she'd given the flowers to a few minutes earlier. Dr. Jackson and Jessie came to stand beside her.

"They need you in trauma room three," a nurse replied. "Pregnant teen. Walked in alone already crowning. No identification. No prenatal care. Unsure of gestation but estimated to be around thirty-three weeks. Dr. Gibbons called for a NICU team."

"And my staff must have been called into the high risk multiple birth scheduled for this afternoon." Triplets, one in distress, being delivered by Cesarean section at twenty-nine weeks. Scarlet removed her lab coat and handed it to Jessie. "Looks like I'm it. Please call the NICU and speak with Ashley," she directed the unit clerk. "Tell her I'm here and to alert Dr. Donaldson and Mac from Respiratory Therapy that I'll have them paged if I need them. And ask her to send down an incubator."

"What can I do to help?" Dr. Jackson asked.

"Would you please have someone turn on the warming table and get me a disposable gown, gloves, and heated towels?"

"Done." He turned to Jessie. "Wait for me in my office. Do. Not. Go. Anywhere."

Scarlet entered the room and introduced herself to the staff, "I'm Scarlet from the NICU."

A young girl with short black hair maybe fifteen or sixteen years old lay on a stretcher. Two nurses held her bare pale legs bent and open. An older heavyset doctor stood between them.

The girl cried out, "It hurts."

Scarlet quickly washed her hands, hurried to the head of the bed and took the girl's hands in hers. "Breathe through the pain," she said. "Like this." She demonstrated.

The girl looked up, her eyes wet with tears, her face red, her expression a mix of pain and fear. "I can't do this," she said.

"You can, and you will," Scarlet answered. "Squeeze my hands as hard as you can. You won't hurt me."

"Here comes another one," she cried out.

And as she squeezed Scarlet's hands, the memory of experiencing this very same situation when she was around this girl's age squeezed Scarlet's heart.

"Bear down and push," the doctor instructed.

"Push, push, push," Scarlet encouraged. "Just like that. You're doing great."

When the contraction ended Scarlet introduced herself, "My name is Scarlet and I'm the nurse who will be taking care of your baby when it's born." She used the corner of the sheet to blot the sweat from the girl's forehead and upper lip. "What's your name?"

The girl hesitated but answered, "Holly."

"Why are you here all alone, Holly?" Scarlet

asked, fearing the answer. "Tell me who to call. A family member? A friend?"

A panicked look overtook her face. "They don't know," she said. "No one can know." Scarlet recalled her own seventeen-year-old desperation, hiding her growing pregnant belly from her high school classmates and family, dealing with the overwhelming, all-consuming fear of someone finding out, of giving birth, and of where she'd go afterwards and how she'd care and provide for her baby. Without a job. Without a high school diploma. Without the help and support of anyone.

How naïve she'd been, actually looking forward to running away, to finally having someone she could love who would love her back.

But that dream had been ripped away when she'd gone into labor months earlier than she'd expected, when her irate, powerful, and medically connected father had accompanied her to one of the many hospitals he worked with, when she'd awoken three days later with little recollection of what'd occurred after her baby had been whisked away other than her weak cry echoing in Scarlet's ears, only to be told her infant had died. According to one of the nurses—who'd had trouble looking her in the eye—she'd been so distraught when she'd been told about her baby's death she'd required sedation, and so as not to upset her further, her father had arranged for private burial. Without allowing Scarlet to see or hold the baby she'd carried inside her body for months, to say goodbye or gain closure.

And her father had never revealed the location of the grave, a secret he and her mother had taken with them to the hereafter eight years ago, leaving Scarlet to always wonder—

"Oh, God. Here comes another one," Holly cried.

"Just like before," Scarlet said, wishing it was possible to bolster this child's strength with some of her own.

"You're doing great," the doctor said at the end of the contraction. Holly flopped back onto the stretcher. "I think one more push should do it."

Holly turned her head to Scarlet, exhausted, her eyes pleading. "Promise me you'll take good care of my baby. Promise me she'll be okay."

A wound so big and so catastrophic it'd taken years to heal broke open deep inside of Scarlet at the memory of her own desperate pleas to the nurses caring for her during delivery, pleas that had fallen on deaf ears. *'I don't want my father in here.' 'I want to see my baby.' 'Please, bring me my baby.'*

"Promise me you'll find her a good home."

Why not Holly's home? *Her.* Wait a minute. "You know it's a girl?" She could only know that if she'd had a prenatal ultrasound. "Who told you it's a girl?" A medical facility would have documentation and contact information.

"I want her named Joey." She ignored Scarlet's question. "I want her to grow up happy, with a family who loves her." She stiffened. "Oh, God. Another one. I'm not ready."

"Yes, you are, Holly. Come on. It's time to have your little girl."

"Let me take over here," Dr. Jackson said, holding up the same type of light blue disposable gown he now wore.

"I've got to get ready to take care of your baby, Holly."

She didn't release Scarlet's hands. "Promise me she'll be okay." Tears streamed down her cheeks. "Promise me."

She couldn't promise that. "I'll do my best," she said. And with a small smile she added, "I'm going to need my hands." Holly loosened her grip.

Scarlet stepped away from the bed to slip into the gown and turn so Dr. Jackson could tie the back. While she donned a mask and gloves, Dr. Jackson did indeed take over for her, talking quietly and supportively while offering direction and praise. Why didn't he show that care with his daughter?

"Don't push," the doctor delivering the baby said.

"What's wrong?" Holly asked, frantic. "I have to push. Get her out."

"The cord is wrapped around the baby's neck," the doctor answered. "Don't. Push."

Dr. Jackson held Holly's hands and instructed her to breathe. "Perfect. You are doing perfect."

After a few tense minutes the doctor delivering the baby said, "Okay, we are good to go, on the next contraction push out your baby."

In no time baby Joey entered the world with a tiny cry of displeasure, her cord was cut, and she'd been handed into Scarlet's waiting towel draped arms. She did a quick assessment and determined it'd be okay to show her to her mom before taking her into the next room. "Do you want to see your baby?" she asked walking up to the head of the bed, knowing sometimes a woman planning to give her baby up for adoption did not.

"Chest...hurts," Holly said, struggling for breath. "Can't...breathe."

"What's happening?" Scarlet asked, holding Joey close.

"Don't know," Dr. Jackson said. "But whatever it is, Dr. Gibbons will handle it. We need to stabilize the baby." He set a large strong hand at her back to guide her toward a side door leading into another room. "The warming table is this way."

"No pulse," the nurse standing by the head of Holly's bed said. "Initiating CPR." She clasped her hands together and began chest compressions.

Scarlet stopped and stared. Please, God. Don't let her die.

"Come." Dr. Jackson urged her forward, pushing open the door. "We need to focus on the baby," he reminded her.

"I know." But that didn't mean she could completely turn off concern for the mother, a young woman she'd connected with for a brief few minutes. Luckily when they reached the warming table Scarlet clicked into auto-nurse, wiping down the too quiet newborn to stimulate her as much as to clean her. "I'm going to need her weight."

"The baby scale was in use," Dr. Jackson said. "Let me go grab it."

When he left the room, Scarlet listened to

Joey's chest to count her heart and respiratory rates. Then she found the equipment she needed and fastened a pulse oximeter to her tiny hand to evaluate her blood oxygen level.

The baby lay on the warmer with her arms and legs flexed, her color pale. Not good.

When Dr. Jackson returned with the scale he placed a disposable cloth over it and Scarlet carefully lifted the naked baby and set her down. "Four point one pounds." Scarlet jotted the number down on a notepad by the warmer and reported the other findings she'd noted there. "Pulse ox ninety. Heart rate one hundred and eighty. Increased respiratory effort. Color pale. Initial Apgar score a five." All of which were abnormal for an infant.

"Let's get a line in to give a bolus of normal saline and get her hooked up to some supplemental oxygen."

While Dr. Jackson inserted a tiny nasal cannula in Joey's nostrils, taped the tubing to her cheeks, and set the flow meter to provide the appropriate level of oxygen, Scarlet started an intravenous in Joey's left arm—noting she didn't flinch or cry.

While she taped it down and immobilized the appendage in an extended position, Dr. Jackson did a quick heel stick to evaluate Joey's blood sugar level.

They worked quickly, quietly and efficiently like they'd been working together for years.

"Blood glucose twenty-five," he reported and began rummaging around a drawer in the warmer until he found the reference card for the recommended dosages for premature infants by weight. "Add a bolus of dextrose." He called out his orders and Scarlet filled the syringes and administered their contents via the newly inserted IV line.

"Come on, Joey," she said, rubbing her thighs in an attempt to perk her up.

The door slammed open and in rolled an incubator being pushed by Cindy. "You okay down here?" she asked.

"Better than expected," Scarlet replied, considering who she'd had to work with. Luckily, Dr. Jackson's reputation as an excellent physician came well-deserved.

"Good." Cindy turned to leave. "The NICU is nuts. I talked to Admissions. Baby Doe," a placeholder name since Holly hadn't shared her last name, "will be going into room forty-two."

"Call Admissions and tell them it's Joey Doe. Holly told me she wanted her baby to be named Joey." And following through on that was the least she could do.

"Roger that." She saluted then walked over to take a look at their soon-to-be new patient. "Too bad about her mom."

"She's…?" Scarlet couldn't continue.

Cindy looked between her and Dr. Jackson and slowly nodded. "I'm sorry. I thought you knew."

Scarlet turned away, held herself tightly, fearing for the first time in years she might cry. For Holly who'd died too young. For Joey now alone in the world. For her own infant and not knowing if she'd suffered, if anyone had cuddled her

close before she'd died, or if she'd been ruth-
lessly given away to strangers while Scarlet lay
in a drug-induced slumber.

"You okay?" Dr. Jackson asked quietly.

Of course she was. Scarlet wasn't new to nursing. Holly wasn't the first of her patients to die.
But there was something about her…"What do
you think happened?"

He shrugged and shook his head. "Some congenital heart defect that couldn't withstand labor
and delivery. A pulmonary embolism. Any number of pre-existing conditions that could have
worsened or arisen during her pregnancy that
we didn't know about. Dr. Gibbons is an excellent doctor. I have total confidence he did all he
could do."

"It wasn't enough."

As if to share her agreement, little Joey Doe
let out a little cry and they both looked down at
their tiny patient. "Her color is improving," Scarlet noted. "And she's more alert."

With skilled, gentle hands, Dr. Jackson examined the increasingly active baby. "Heart rate down to one hundred and twenty. I'd give her a second Apgar score of seven."

Not a perfect ten, but improved. Scarlet documented it in her notes.

"She's stable enough for transport up to the NICU," Dr. Jackson said. Then he helped her get Joey situated in the incubator.

"After I get her settled in I'll access her ER file and enter my documentation."

"If you run into any trouble, let me know." He held out his hand and she shook it. "Thanks for the help."

"Anytime." She went to remove her hand from his grip but he held it there.

"We need to talk about Jessie," Dr. Jackson said. So serious. Did the man ever smile? According to Jessie, no he did not.

Scarlet took a moment to admire his tall, athletic build and short brown hair mixed with a hint of grey at his temples. He had a look of confidence and prestige she would have found very attractive on someone else. "No," Scarlet said, looking to where he held her hand. "*You* need to talk to *your* daughter." She looked up at him. "And here's a helpful hint to improving communication between the two of you." She yanked her hand back. "Stop comparing her to the perfect little boy you used to be. Just because you loved swimming and boating and all things water when you were a child, doesn't mean she does."

Later that night Lewis stood in his designer kitchen, eyeing the modern stainless steel handle on the high-end black cabinet that contained the bottles of wine he'd kept at the ready in case any of his dates wanted a glass, and considered uncorking one. Although he wasn't in the habit of drinking alone, it'd been the kind of day followed by the kind of night that warranted a little alcohol consumption to facilitate a return to his pre-Jessie level of calm.

But Lewis Jackson had never turned to alcohol to drown his problems before, and he refused

to start now. He was a problem solver, a thinker
and a fixer. And to do those things he required
a clear head.

Since his daughter had taken up permanent residence in the loft guestroom, he tended to avoid
the living area below after she went to sleep. So
he walked down the hall to his bedroom, the
smooth hardwood floors cool beneath his bare
feet, the central air maintaining the perfect air
temperature, his two bedroom luxury condo dec-
orated to his exact specifications for style, comfort and function. And yet his home no longer
brought him the welcoming serenity it once had.

Jessie hadn't said more than a handful of
words—all of them monosyllabic—to him since
they'd left the hospital, even after he'd insisted
they eat their takeout grilled chicken Caesar sal-
ads together in the kitchen for a change. What an
uncomfortable meal that'd been. Jessie, staring
down at her plate, moving the chicken around
with her fork. Lewis, trying to engage her in conversation, to offer reassurance about her trip to

Lake George, to find out more about her relationship with Scarlet Miller, and, for the hundredth time, to gain some insight into the functioning of the pre-pubescent female mind. A booby-trapped labyrinth of erratic and illogical thought processes he could not seem to navigate through, despite successful completion of several child psychology classes and licensure as a pediatrician.

After nine arduous months of trying, and failing his daughter at every crisis, Lewis gave in to the cold, hard fact: He could not do it alone.

And yet again, an image of Scarlet Miller popped into his head. A pretty yet unfriendly woman and a skilled professional, who, he'd found out on further inquiry, received high praise and much respect from her peers and upper management. But at the moment, all that mattered to him was her relationship with his daughter.

He reached into his pocket, pulled out the slip of paper he'd stashed there earlier, and glanced at his watch. A few minutes after eleven o'clock.

It was too late to call, but his need to talk to her, to get answers and beg for her assistance over-rode common phone etiquette. After hours and hours spent considering his options, Lewis had come to the conclusion Scarlet Miller was his key to deciphering Jessie's passive-aggressive be-havior and learning her secrets, to understanding her and starting a productive dialogue between them, so he could help her, so he could, please God, find something about her to love.

Lewis picked up his phone and dialed.

After a few rings a groggy female voice an-swered, "Hello?"

Great, he'd woke her up. And the last thing he wanted to do was anger his best hope for achieving a healthy, positive relationship with his daughter. He cleared his throat. "Hi. It's Lewis."

"I'm sorry. You have the wrong number."

"Wait. Is this Scarlet Miller?" he rushed to ask before she disconnected the call, and before it registered that if she hung up, she'd never know he was the inconsiderate louse who'd woken her.

Well…unless she had caller ID. Then he'd no doubt come off looking even worse.

"Yes," she answered.

"It's me. Lewis Jackson. Jessie's dad."

"Is she okay?" Scarlet sounded instantly awake. "Did something happen?"

Lewis liked and appreciated her concern for his daughter. "No, she's fine. Upstairs asleep." At least as far as he knew. And since he'd learned the hard way never to assume Jessie was where she was supposed to be, Lewis walked to the doorway, poked his head into the hallway to con-firm it was indeed eavesdropper-free, then closed and locked his bedroom door, just in case it didn't stay that way.

"How did you get this number?" Scarlet asked. "I'm sure I didn't give it to you. And I doubt Jes-sie would have shared it."

Okay, time for some fast talking. "I just hap-pened to come across the card you'd given to Jes-sie," after searching for it in her backpack and pocketbook while she was in the shower—bad, reprehensible father—"while checking her plethora of pockets before putting her pants in the wash," he lied. "I took it as a sign I should call you."

Silence.

"Hello?" he asked.

She let out a decidedly feminine, sultry sounding moan which made him question, "Am I interrupting something?"

"No." She did it again. "I don't typically talk on the phone when I'm in bed. I'm trying to find a comfortable position."

And just like that, with the mere mention she was in bed, without-sex-for-nine-long-months-brain overtook concerned-father-brain with an enticing visual of her luscious body. A comfortable position came to mind. Scarlet spread out on top of satin sheets. Naked. Waiting.

His sex-starved body went hard.

"Soooo, *you* called me," she said. "What can I do for you?"

A loaded question if ever there was one. Because right this instant he wanted her to talk dirty, to touch herself and tell him all about it, to describe her aroused nipples and slick… Lord help him. Prolonged abstinence had effectively eradicated his ability to engage in casual night-time conversation with a woman. From bedroom to bedroom. And if he took a few small steps, from bed to bed. And from out of nowhere, the idea of phone sex popped into his head.

"Hello. Everything okay over there?"

Totally disgusted with himself, Lewis rubbed his hand over his face and let out a breath. "A bad day followed by a bad night combined with a non-existent sex life since my daughter came to live with me and I am conjuring up totally inappropriate visuals of you, a woman I have known for less than twenty-four hours, at the simple mention of you getting comfortable in bed. In my defense, you were making some very sexy noises a moment ago, so I hold you partly responsible. But I assure you, when I picked up the phone to make this call my intentions were purely G-rated."

"And now what are they?" she teased.

"Let's just say, the next time you see me you owe me a slap across the face, because I totally deserve it."

Turned out she had a sexy laugh, too.

He shifted in the recliner to relieve some of the pressure in his pants. Not good. Scarlet Miller was not the woman to slake his lust. He needed her to fix things between him and Jessie and would not risk anything interfering with his top priority. "Please accept my sincerest apologies."

"Accepted, but not necessary," she said. "For the record, you could pass for sexy on the phone too."

"You are not helping."

"Do you want to know what I'm wearing?" she taunted him.

"Absolutely not," he lied.

"I could—"

"Stop it."

"Fine," she said. "But you started it."

"And I'm going to finish it." Only because someone had to. "I called to talk about Jessie.

To try to sweet talk you into sharing some more helpful hints on improving communication between us, because the direct approach is not working."

"Too bad. That's the closest I've ever come to having phone sex."

Did he detect a hint of disappointment? "Oddly enough, me, too," he admitted. And why did he feel so comfortable sharing that tidbit with a woman he hardly knew?

"You know you're putting me in a tough spot," Scarlet said, her voice serious. "I can't betray things Jessie has told me in confidence. She really needs a friend to talk to, and right now I'm it. It took me a long time to get her to open up."

He wanted to ask how she'd managed that, but decided to start with, "Would you at least tell me how you met?"

She took so long to answer Lewis had started to worry she wouldn't.

"That I can do." It sounded like she repositioned herself in bed. Again. "I work late on Tuesdays and Thursdays to spend some time with my night staff. So I take a break at three."

"Right around when I send Jessie down to get a snack after school."

"The cafeteria isn't usually busy at that time so I noticed her, always sitting there by herself with that 'don't talk to me' look."

Lewis hated that look.

"I saw a lot of my thirteen-year-old self in Jessie. Mad at the world. Too much time alone and unsupervised. Do you honestly think she's safe wandering around alone in a city hospital for hours waiting for you to get off work?"

Lewis did not appreciate the censure in her tone. She had no idea how hard he'd tried. "That was her doing not mine. I told her what would happen if she made one more babysitter quit. And she's not supposed to be wandering around alone," he pointed out maybe a little too forcefully. *Calm it down.* "She's supposed to be in my office doing her homework." Except his little Houdini always managed to sneak out without anyone seeing then show up hours later when it was time to go home. "What do you suggest I do? Let her stay at my condo all alone until I get home, like she'd prefer? Maybe some thirteen-year-olds are ready for that. But in my opinion Jessie isn't." And his opinion was the one that mattered.

"I agree," Scarlet said, surprising him. "But it's a moot point since I've got her spending her afternoons up in the NICU wing now."

"Where?" Why?

"We have a family lounge. It's geared towards the siblings of our babies who are often over-looked while their parents focus their attention on their sick infant. So we made them a special place with video games, toys, computers to do their homework, a television and a kid-friendly library that holds everything from picture books to young adult novels. Jessie comes up to read every afternoon."

Jessie liked to read? They actually had some-thing in common? Yet in the nine months she'd been living with him he'd never seen her with a book.

"I'm sorry. I assumed she told you."

"Aside from mostly no's and the occasional yes, she hardly speaks to me. I do get a lot of shrugs, exasperated breaths and eye rolls, though. And when she does surprise me with a full sentence, it's usually to tell me how much she hates me, that she knows I don't want her, or that she wishes I'd died instead of her mother." Then he'd rather she'd just stayed quiet.

"She has a lot of anger."

Rightly so. But, "It's been nine months. Shouldn't it be dissipating a bit by now?"

"If only time was all she needed."

"Tell me what she needs. I'll do anything."

Silence.

"Please," Lewis said. "If you want me to beg, I will." He slid to the edge of the recliner, fully prepared to drop to his knees. "I am that desperate."

Silence.

Lewis started to lose hope that Scarlet would be the panacea he needed.

Then she spoke. "If you can slip up to the NICU family lounge around four o'clock tomorrow you'll see a different side of Jessie. One that I'm sure will make you proud."

An opportunity he would not miss. "I'll be there."

"She can't know I told you. Say you came up to check on baby Joey, and my staff told you where to find me."

"Will do."

"I'm giving you an opportunity for a positive interaction with your daughter, Lewis. Don't screw it up."

CHAPTER THREE

AT THREE-THIRTY on Wednesday afternoon, washed up and gowned, Scarlet opened Joey's incubator. The baby refused to suck so Dr. Donaldson had placed a naso-gastric tube for feeding. "Hey there, you sweet little girl," she said softly so as not to startle her. Joey blinked her eyes and stretched in response to Scarlet's voice.

Good.

Scarlet pressed her index finger against the baby's tiny palm so she could grab onto it. "I promised your mommy I'd take good care of you." A promise she intended to keep. She repositioned her many tubes and carefully wrapped her in a baby blanket. "We need to get you drinking from a bottle so you can grow up big and strong." She lifted her and slowly moved to the rocker two steps away, careful not to pull on the many lines connected to her.

Once situated, she began to rock. Joey made a contented little moan and cuddled into her. "Don't get too comfortable," she warned and picked up the little bottle beside her. "We've got some work to do."

Since taking on a management role, Scarlet missed providing direct care to the NICU's tiny patients. "Open up." She rubbed the special nipple along Joey's bottom lip and squeezed out a drop of formula.

So far the NICU social worker hadn't been able to come up with any information on Holly. Police were reviewing missing persons reports and Holly's post mortem picture had been faxed to OB/GYN offices, prenatal clinics and schools within a thirty mile radius of the hospital. Scarlet couldn't help wondering why Holly didn't want her family to know about the baby. For fear of their reaction to her pregnancy? Shame? Scarlet could relate. But what if there was more? What if her home environment wasn't safe for her baby? If her parents were unfit to raise a child, like Scarlet's had been? Or if someone abusive would have access to the baby?

And what if Holly was never identified and her family never found? What then? Joey would wind up in an over-burdened, flawed child welfare system. Helpless and vulnerable.

Promise me she'll be okay. Promise me you'll find her a good home. A dead mother's final plea to Scarlet, who had absolutely no control over Joey's placement.

Unless she sought to adopt her.

An absurd notion, considering Scarlet didn't spend enough time at home to keep a pet alive. How could she work the hours she did and effectively care for an infant? The question that'd been weighing on her mind for months as her biological clock beat out the second by second withering of her reproductive organs.

Baby Joey fell asleep in her arms and Scarlet savored a few minutes of peace in the darkened quiet room, loving the feel of Joey in her arms. Like she did every time she held a NICU patient, she tried to convince herself. But no, it was different with Joey, maybe because Joey's mom had entrusted her daughter to Scarlet. Maybe because Holly reminded her so much of herself, and Joey, now all alone in the world, had wound up like Scarlet's baby when she'd been purposely chemically incapacitated.

Regardless, Scarlet had a vested interest in Joey and would do whatever she could to assure the child a bright, happy and safe future.

Grandma Sadie, one of their volunteer cuddlers, came in to Joey's room and whispered, "Linda told me to come relieve you."

Grandma Sadie had been in Scarlet's first volunteer cuddler orientation class, back when she'd implemented the program four years ago. Research showed preemies benefited from human touch and interaction. And cuddlers filled the gap when exhausted parents needed a break, or when babies, like Joey, had no family to love them.

She glanced at her watch. "Perfect timing." Since she had to get over to the family lounge before Lewis arrived.

Scarlet busied herself by re-shelving books and putting away toys. Then she spoke with a few moms sitting at a table in the back of the room, enjoying a rest and some coffee while Jessie held 'story time' to occupy their five little girls who ranged in age from two to five. They sat in a circle on the floor, each taking a turn in Jessie's lap while she read their selection.

When Lewis entered the room, Scarlet motioned for him to be quiet and come to stand beside her.

So engrossed in her task, Jessie didn't notice his arrival as she made an exaggerated honking noise that sent the little girls into a pile of gigglers.

Lewis watched his daughter, his face a mix of awe and disbelief.

"Jessie holds 'story time' around four o'clock

every afternoon," she whispered. "The moms meet up for a few precious minutes of adult conversation, while your daughter gives each of their children some special attention." Scarlet looked up at him. "She's really something special."

Jessie finished one book and, with a big smile on her face, accepted a kiss on the cheek from the girl in her lap. Then the circle shifted, the next little girl climbed in her lap and she began to read again.

"I can't believe it," Lewis whispered, his eyes locked on Jessie. "She's actually smiling."

"She has a beautiful smile," Scarlet pointed out.

Lewis turned to her. "This is the first time I've ever seen it."

"Dad," Jessie walked up beside them. "What are you doing here?"

"I'm sorry. I didn't mean to interrupt," Lewis said. "I came up to check on the baby born in the ER yesterday, and the secretary at the desk told me I'd find Scarlet in here."

Good man, very convincing.

Jessie stood defiant, ready to do battle. "If you're going to yell at me please do it outside. I don't want to upset the girls." Who sat watching Jessie, still in a circle, awaiting her return.

Lewis went rigid. "Why do you think I'm going to yell?"

"Because you always yell."

Lewis looked close to lashing out so Scarlet touched his arm to stop him. "Always is one of those words you need to use carefully," Scarlet cautioned Jessie. "It's rare someone *always* does something."

"You don't know my dad," Jessie replied with an eye roll, and Scarlet couldn't keep from smiling.

"If I was going to say anything," Lewis said. "It'd be how nice it was to see you smiling for a change, and how proud I am to know you're spending your time helping out here."

Jessie looked stunned.

One of the moms came over. "Is this your dad?"

she asked Jessie who nodded hesitantly as if embarrassed.

The woman put her arm around Jessie's shoulders. "You have a gem of a daughter." She looked in the direction of Lewis's name badge and added, "Dr. Jackson. You've done a wonderful job with her."

Lewis answered, "Thank you." Then he turned to look at Jessie. "I wish I could take the credit, but it was all her mother."

Jessie ran from the room.

Lewis and Scarlet caught up with her by the elevators and she turned on her father. "Why are you being so nice?" Jessie asked her voice full of accusation. "You hated my mom, and you hate me."

A couple exited the elevator, avoiding eye contact as they passed by.

"Honey, I have never hated your mother, and I don't hate you," Lewis said, impressing Scarlet with his calm. "I let my anger and disappointment at having to pick you up at the police station get the better of me yesterday, and I am deeply sorry for what I said."

Jessie stood there, her arms crossed tightly over her mid-section, looking down at the ground.

"Now that I know where you're spending your afternoons, I can stop worrying," Lewis said quietly.

"I'm sorry I didn't tell you," Jessie offered, still not looking up.

It was a start. But with the Memorial Day weekend of doom fast approaching, was it enough to get Lewis and Jessie talking about what they needed to talk about? Probably not. Which meant Scarlet had to figure out a way to intercede without Jessie finding out.

Later that night, after spending more time thinking about Lewis and his daughter than sleeping, Scarlet settled on what she'd do. Of course it'd taken until well after midnight to finally make up her mind—the reason she sat in the far corner of the mostly deserted hospital cafeteria hours before her lunch break, waiting for Lewis.

He walked in and went directly to the coffee dispensers, giving Scarlet time to play voyeur, watching from afar, admiring his long legs, short hair, and good looks. The man made basic green scrubs look like upscale attire. Clean and neatly pressed. And dare she add, pleasingly filled out.

No wonder she'd heard his name bandied about by so many of her single co-workers.

She skimmed up his legs, to his narrow waist and wide chest, to his smiling face, to his eyes staring straight at her.

Busted.

She smiled back and waved.

He paid the cashier and headed toward her. "You like what you see?" he asked with the cocky smile of a man who knew he looked good, pulling out the chair across from her at the small, two-person table along the wall.

"Actually," she took a sip of coffee, playing it cool. "Just pondering the age old question of boxers or briefs."

He leaned in close.

She added straight white teeth, clean shaven, and a hint of expensive cologne to his growing list of unsettlingly pleasing attributes.

"Use your imagination," he whispered.

Oh he did not want her to go there. Too late. She closed her eyes and pretended to imagine his naked form with various undergarments. Okay. So she didn't totally pretend. When she opened her eyes to find him studying her, she flashed her sweetest smile and said, "Commando it is."

He laughed out loud.

"Suffice it to say, I no longer owe you a slap across the face." She blew out a breath and fanned herself. "We are now even." Come to find out he had a beautiful smile, so much like Jessie's.

"You make me forget I'm the father of an impressionable teenage girl."

"You know being a parent does not sentence you to a life of celibacy. Why don't you pull up your date book and call one of your five star babes to take the edge off. It'll calm you down.

I'm happy to take Jess to dinner and a movie."
She smiled back. "Your treat, of course."

He rested his elbows on the table and leaned
in close. "Why is it we never met *before* Jessie
came into my life?"

Oh that was easy. "Probably because I don't
dress to attract male attention, my boobs don't
enter a room before I do, and I've never gone to
O'Malley's after work intent on finding a sexy
doctor to go home with." And she had a brain
and self-respect and stayed away from men
who didn't put any effort into getting to know a
woman before making a play to get her into bed.

His smile grew even bigger. "You think I'm
sexy?"

And full of himself. "Based on your reputation, I think it's safe to say certain women find
you sexy. Or else they simply put up with you in
a desperate attempt to snag themselves a doctor husband." She shrugged. "It's a discussion
for another day." She looked at her watch. "Unless you'd like to continue rather than talk about

Jessie, who is the reason I asked you to meet me here. Your choice. I've got rounds with the neonatologist in fifteen minutes."

That knocked the cocky grin from his lips.

Good.

"What can you tell me about Jessie's mom?" she asked, hoping to get him to figure out Jessie's issues on his own, so she could avoid having to come right out and tell him.

He took a sip of coffee before answering. "There's not much to tell. She was a barista at a coffee shop around the corner from my medical school. We dated a few times, and by dated," he looked at her pointedly without apology or regret, "I really mean got together for sex. When she put pressure on me to spend more time with her, we fought. She became a distraction so I broke it off," he said matter-of-factly. "I needed to focus on my studies. So I found another coffee shop and she, according to a ranting message left on my answering machine, found a man who appreciated her—likely one more easily manipulated by her histrionics. After that I never saw, spoke with, or to be honest, thought about her again until I received a call from her attorney nine months ago informing me she'd died and I had a twelve-year-old daughter."

The news of his situation had spread through the hospital like pink eye in a room full of toddlers. "That must have come as quite a shock."

"You have no idea."

At age sixteen she'd found out she was pregnant and had no recollection of having sex. At seventeen she'd given birth only to wake up to find her baby gone. She had some idea.

"Well this entire Lake George vacation mess could have been avoided if you'd taken the time to get to know Jessie's mother before you slept with her."

"Trust me," he said. "If I'd have taken the time to get to know her, I would not have slept with her."

For some reason that struck her as funny.

"Enjoying this are you?"

"No." She shook her head. "Okay. Maybe a little. But moving on." Since plan A didn't work, time to move on to plan B. "Let's play doctor."

He looked around then leaned in and whispered. "To do the game justice we'll need some privacy."

"You are unbelievable," Scarlet reprimanded him. "I am trying to clue you in to Jessie's fears about Lake George. But maybe it's not as important to you as I'd thought. And since there are plenty of more important things I could be doing." She pushed back her chair.

"Wait." He grabbed her hand to stop her from standing. "I'm sorry," he said, sounding sincere. "I can't help it. There's something about you." He studied her as if trying to figure out what. "I'll behave. I promise." He held up his right hand, as if that made his words more believable.

"Okay, then." Scarlet slid her chair back under the table. "You're the doctor. I'm going to tell you a hypothetical situation and you're going to tell me what you think."

"Hypothetical," he clarified with a tilt of his head and one raised eyebrow.

"Yes." She nodded. "Purely hypothetical."

"Got it."

"A woman has a near-death drowning experience as a little girl and grows up with a crippling fear of the water. She has a daughter. The daughter grows up under the mother's watchful eye, never allowed in the ocean, a lake or a swimming pool, and therefore never given the opportunity to learn how to swim. Do you think it's reasonable to assume the daughter may also develop a fear of water?"

He smacked his forehead with the heel of his hand. "And all this time I've been playing up how much fun she'd have at the lake, jumping off the dock in the backyard," he said. "Boating. Tubing. Riding wave runners. I've no doubt traumatized her. Why didn't she tell me?" He looked at Scarlet for the answer.

"It's been seventeen years since I've spent any time in a thirteen-year-old's mixed up mind, but maybe she's embarrassed. Or she doesn't want you to blame her mom. Or she somehow thinks you'll belittle her fear or force her to deal with it. I honestly don't know."

Lewis sat there, staring at the table.

"What are you going to do now that you've taken the time to really put some thought into why Jessie doesn't want to go to Lake George and you've come up with the possibility she may be scared of the water," Scarlet asked. "And might I say good job of coming up with it totally on your own and without the help of anyone else."

Determined eyes met hers. "When we get home tonight I'm going to sit Jessie down and we're going to discuss her exact reasons for not wanting to go to Lake George. And if she doesn't bring up a fear of water or an inability to swim, I will find a way to work it into the conversation."

Finally. "I think that's a wonderful idea."

The words weren't fully out of her mouth when someone came to stand beside their table. Scarlet looked up to see Linda from the NICU, looking down at where Lewis still held her hand in his.

"Well what have we here?" Linda asked with a gleam in her gossip-mongering, match-making eyes.

Not good.

"Must I spend my Saturday afternoon in this touristy hell that is Times Square?" Scarlet complained as they maneuvered along the crowded sidewalk. Lewis kept an eye on Jessie who stopped to look at scarves laid out on a street vendor's table.

"Stop being a cynical New Yorker," he chided delighted to be away from the hospital and his condo, to be outside on a beautiful sun-shiny spring day on his first fun New York City excursion with his daughter. And having Scarlet along upped the enjoyment factor significantly.

"Technically I'm a Jersey girl."

Maybe so, but she looked the part of a chic New York City woman in her wedge-heeled open toed

sandals, which displayed some perfectly manicured bright red toe nails, a pair of trendy knee-
length cargo shorts that sat low on her hips, and a
clingy red tank that accentuated her flat abdomen
and small—although not too small—breasts. An
over-sized red leather bag slung over her shoulder, a sleek ponytail fastened with a fancy silver
clip, and silver hoop earrings finished off her
very fashionable, very appealing look.

"Remind me again why I'm here?" she asked.

Jessie didn't buy a scarf, but she did purchase
a pretzel. He watched her count her change like
he'd told her and put the money into her front
pocket. "Because you told Jessie she could call
you anytime for any reason."

Scarlet snapped her fingers. "Right. And she
wanted *me* to take her shopping for a bathing suit
and some new vacation clothes."

After his conversation with Scarlet, Lewis had
carefully, patiently and tactfully worked to pry
the truth out of Jessie. And once she'd opened up
to him, months of accumulated fears, concerns

and tears had come pouring out. They'd talked for hours, and before bed Jessie had actually said, "Thanks, dad." His first amiable 'dad' followed by his very first hug and kiss good night from his daughter. A moment he would never forget. And though he'd never admit it to anyone, he'd teared up after she'd left the room, overwhelmed with relief. And hope.

"Yet somehow *we* wound up in Times Square. If *I'm* the one taking her to lunch and shopping," Scarlet peered up at him from the corners of her eyes, "Why are *you* here again?"

"Because I'm financing this little clothes shopping expedition, so I get the right of final approval."

Scarlet's smile did something tingly to his insides. "Oh you think so?" she asked.

He was the father. He knew so.

In an attempt to avoid a very persistent man trying to hand her a leaflet of some sort, Scarlet bumped into him and tripped. Lewis caught her around her narrow waste. "We're not interested," he said firmly and the man retreated.

"Why's that guy out in public in his underwear?" Jessie went up on her tiptoes and strained her neck to see around a group that'd gathered on the sidewalk. "And a cowboy hat and boots? And why are people taking their picture with him?"

"Let's keep walking," Lewis said, steering Jessie and Scarlet away.

"He does it to attract attention to himself so he can make some money by charging people who want to take a picture with him," Scarlet explained. "Tourists spend money on the craziest things."

Lewis watched the huge jumbotron on the side of a building to find the spot where the cameras were aimed. "Hold on." He turned Jessie. "Look up."

She did. "Hey." She waved both arms over her head and jumped up and down. "That's me."

"And me," Scarlet said with a big smile as she jumped and waved, too.

Lewis bent to talk into Scarlet's ear, noticing she smelled as good as she looked. "How touristy of you."

She stuck out her tongue at him then looped her arm through Jessie's. "Come on. This store has some great clothes."

As much as Lewis hated Jessie's baggie black garb—that'd turned to be hand-me-downs from a neighbor since her mom had been too sick to work and couldn't afford new clothes—Lewis was not at all a fan of Jessie's revealing, burgeoning-figure-hugging choices. "No," he said again and Jessie stormed back to the dressing room. Unfortunately it seemed last night's parental epiphany did not mean smooth sailing from then on.

"You know you're going to have to give a little," Scarlet said, remaining by his side instead of following Jessie.

"That shirt was too tight." He swallowed. "Do you think she needs a…" God he hated this. Daughters should not have breasts for boys who will soon be men to look at. Suddenly baggie black attire didn't seem all that bad.

Scarlet smiled, enjoying his angst a little too much. "Bra?" she asked. "Do I think your daughter needs a bra?" she teased.

"Ssshhh," he said. "Keep your voice down."

She didn't. "Tell you what I'm gonna do," she said like some cheesy salesman trying to sweeten the deal. "If you let Jessie get three outfits and two bathing suits of her choice, I will accompany her to Macy's." She cupped her hands at the sides of her mouth and whispered, "For some bras."

"No V-neck shirts and no bikinis," Lewis clarified.

"If you get stipulations then so do I. I'm thinking I'll suggest she get padded bras to double her bust size."

Witch. "Okay. She can pick from the last batch of stuff she tried on." Which thankfully didn't contain any of the hideously trampy items of clothing Jessie had tried to convince him to consider at the onset of this shopping nightmare.

"Deal." She held out her hand.

He shook it.

"You'll get through this," she said. "Tight shirts and bras are nothing." She waved a flippant hand. "Just wait until she gets her period."

Lewis thought he might throw up right there by the girls denim shorts rack. As a pediatrician he didn't hesitate to discuss breast development, menstruation, and birth control with his patients and/or their nervous parents. But the role of father caring for a developing teenage daughter had taken him into new territory. Had Jessie already gotten her period? Doubtful since he didn't have any feminine supplies in the house and she hadn't asked him to buy any. Had anyone had 'the talk' with her? Did she know what to expect? And what about safe sex? And sexually transmitted diseases?

He now had a vividly clear understanding of parental apprehension and avoidance when discussing reproductive matters with their children.

Pain typical of an ulcer started to burn through the lining in his stomach.

His doctor self knew what had to be done.

His father self would rather preach the pros of maintaining virginity until marriage.

"He looks pale," Jessie said, standing in front of him with her arms full of clothes.

"Men often do when shopping for clothes with women." Scarlet looked up at him with deceptively innocent eyes and smiled. "You feeling okay, papa bear?"

"You are a mean woman," he said so only she'd hear.

"Nah," she said. "If you're nice to me, maybe I'll handle 'the talk'" she made air quotations around 'the talk', "for you."

A total father copout, but thank you! "Lunch is on me," Lewis said, his vigor returning. "Then we'll go to Macy's to buy Scarlet a nice little gift for accompanying us today," he said to Jessie.

They found a little Italian bistro on 46th Street whose posted menu appealed to them all and squeezed into the last available corner booth, Jessie and all her bags on one side, Scarlet and Lewis on the other. When the waiter came to take their drink order Lewis asked Scarlet, "Would you like to share a bottle of wine?" Maybe bra shopping wouldn't be so bad with a nice relaxing buzz.

"No thank you," she said to him. Then she turned to the waiter. "Just water for me, please."

After ordering a soda Jessie said, "Scarlet doesn't drink alcohol, Dad."

"But don't let me stop you from having," Scarlet added quickly.

Lewis decided on an iced tea.

"You don't have to tell him why," Jessie said very serious. "What we say between us stays between us."

"It's not something I share with everyone I meet," Scarlet said. "But it's not a secret, either."

Jessie jumped at the chance to share the reason. "When Scarlet was sixteen she went to a party where the kids were drinking alcohol," Jessie said in horror. "She drank too and got so drunk she passed out."

"I hope you have a good reason for discussing your drunken teenage exploits with my daughter," Lewis said.

Scarlet turned to face him, her eyes met his. "Obviously alcohol impaired my ability to make good decisions because a few weeks later I found out I was pregnant."

She watched him, so Lewis was careful to maintain a neutral expression. He knew he should say something, but what? I'm sorry? How horrible? What happened to the baby?

"That's why kids shouldn't drink alcohol," Jessie said, taking the pressure off of him by filling the silence. "Because it makes them do stupid things they don't remember doing. I'm never drinking alcohol even after I turn twenty-one." She took her soda from the waiter and pulled the paper tip off of the straw.

"Good girl," he said, knowing a thirteen-year-old's declaration of long-term sobriety could be recanted without his knowledge at any time as she moved toward adulthood.

Jessie took a sip of soda then said, "Scarlet's baby is the reason the two of us met."

Very interesting.

Scarlet stared at her water glass, sliding her fingers through the droplets of condensation on the outside. If he wasn't mistaken, a hint of a blush stained her cheeks.

"Jessie, I don't think Scarlet is comfortable with you telling me all this." Even though he wanted to hear more.

"No," Scarlet looked at Jessie. "It's okay. Go on." She glanced at him. "Might as well get it all out." She turned back to Jessie. "It's not good to keep things from your dad."

Later, he'd thank her for that.

"The nurses told Scarlet her baby had died."

Scarlet jumped in to add, "Which is why I decided when I grew up I'd become a nurse who specializes in caring for premature infants."

And from what Lewis had heard and witnessed first-hand, she did a phenomenal job of it.

"But since her father was totally evil and wouldn't let her see her baby and refused to tell her where he'd had the baby buried, she started to wonder what if the baby had really survived?"

If the topic of conversation had been fiction rather than fact, Lewis would have smiled at Jessie's story-telling, wide-eyed and full of intrigue.

"I know it sounds ridiculous." Scarlet picked up the story. "But what if my dad had my baby transferred to another hospital and arranged for her to be adopted? Which, if you knew my dad, you'd know was something he was fully capable of pulling off, considering he also managed to make all documentation from my hospital stay, including any record of the birth, death, or transfer of my daughter, mysteriously disappear. And he did it without any remorse at all to save himself the embarrassment of having an unwed teenage mother for a daughter." Anger seeped into her voice and Lewis felt her stiffen beside him.

How horrible to have endured so much trauma at such a young age. He moved his knee to touch hers in a show of support that seemed to relax her.

"Anyway," Scarlet went on. "If my daughter is in fact alive, she'd be about Jessie's age. And when we met I told Jessie I'd hope if someone saw *my* daughter looking as sad and lonely as she did, they'd take the time to talk to her, and try to cheer her up, and see if there was anything they could do to help her."

"Which is what Scarlet did for me," Jessie said.

"And I am so glad she did," Lewis said, turning to Scarlet. "I'm sorry about your daughter, but words cannot express how thankful I am for the kindness you've shown to mine." Scarlet Miller had a true compassionate soul beneath her tough, joking exterior.

"No biggie." She shrugged off his heartfelt thanks, seeming uncomfortable with the attention. "What do you think happened to our waiter?" She looked down at her menu. "I'm starving."

He allowed the change of topic, but someday soon, when Jessie wasn't around, they'd talk more about his appreciation for all she'd done for Jessie and for him. And he kind of looked forward to getting her alone. Scarlet Miller was fast becoming a woman he wanted to get to know much better.

In Macy's Scarlet said, "If you'll excuse me and Jessie, I have some shopping to do up in the lingerie department." She shooed him away. "Go shop for man things. We'll meet you by women's shoes in half an hour."

If there were any way he could have done it without Jessie seeing, and without getting slapped, he would have kissed Scarlet right then and there.

Forty-five minutes later they appeared, Scarlet carrying a Macy's bag, Jessie empty-handed.

"Did you find what you needed?" he asked. *Please say yes.*

"Yup," she held up a bag he hoped contained Jessie's new undergarments.

"This is for you." He handed her the biggest box of chocolates he could find in the store. "Thank you for coming with us today."

"Wow." Scarlet took the box. "The fat cells in my thighs are vibrating with excitement in anticipation of room to expand."

"I heard how much you and your staff like chocolate," he said, referring to the box they'd devoured before it could be redirected to his new clerk.

"That we do." She smiled. He liked making her smile, liked the way her smiles made him feel. "Thank you, from all of us. But in the future, you don't need to buy me things to spend time with you and Jess. I had fun today."

"Me, too." Jessie hugged Scarlet.

Lewis did, too. In fact today had been the most fun he'd had in months. Even with talk of periods and bras.

When they exited Macy's Lewis asked Scarlet,

"Where are you headed from here? You want to share a cab?"

"Nah." She held up her Metro card. "I'm going to hop a bus to the hospital. I want to stop by to visit Joey before I head home."

"Is there a problem?"

She shook her head. "No."

As Lewis watched Scarlet's appealing form walk away, he realized he was sorry to see her go. And as he raised his hand to hail a cab his mind went to work on creating a reason to see her again soon.

CHAPTER FOUR

"FANCY MEETING YOU here," Lewis greeted Scarlet with a big handsome smile as she exited the elevator on her way to the cafeteria.

"A big coincidence indeed on account of it's Tuesday and you now know I meet Jessie in the cafeteria on Tuesdays and Thursdays around three," she replied, not letting her happiness at seeing him show. In an unexpected turn of events, she'd been looking forward to the next time their paths would cross. And hoping it'd be sooner rather than later.

"I walked her over." He held up a cup of coffee. "Then I waited, hoping to see you."

How sweet.

"I need a favor," he said.

Not so sweet after all. She tried to walk around him.

He stepped in front of her. "For Jessie. One

more and I'm done," he promised. "Then I won't bother you again."

Well forget about the fun they'd had on Saturday, and the signs of a friendship forming between them—that she'd obviously misinterpreted, and the unwanted stirrings of attraction that were totally his fault. All Lewis Jackson wanted from her was help with his daughter. "Lucky me," she said. "One more favor and you'll be done with me. I will have exhausted my usefulness to you, and I didn't even have to take off my clothes."

She pushed past him.

"Oh no you don't." He draped his arm around her shoulders, guiding her, rather firmly, to the quiet back hallway before releasing her. "What's wrong?"

Scarlet adjusted her lab coat. "This must be a whopper for you to manhandle me into listening."

"Why are you mad at me?" he asked, looking truly confused.

Because maybe it'd be nice for a man, one man, any man, to see her as more than a neighbor to get his mail while he's out of town, or a competent professional nurse managing the NICU, or a resource for parenting his teenage daughter. Maybe it'd be nice to be noticed and appreciated as a woman, someone nice to spend time with and not bad to look at, maybe even a little sexy in the right outfit and dim lighting.

"What did I do?"

"Nothing," she said. "Stressful day. Overreaction. Let's move on. What's the favor?"

"Did you *want* to take your clothes off?" he asked seriously. "Tell me where and when and I will happily and enthusiastically join you."

Two weeks ago she'd have fired off a sarcastic comeback meant to shut him down. No, she did not want to earn a place on his long list of meaningless one-night-stands or have her name tossed into the hospital's gossip channels as his latest conquest. But now, things weren't so clear. He was different than she'd first thought. A caring doctor. A nice guy. A father trying to be a better parent. Maybe—

Loud male voices interrupted her thoughts seconds before two men turned the corner into the back hallway.

"Damn you, Cade," the older of the two men said, pushing the other man up against the wall. "Do you hear what's being said about me? People are questioning my integrity and my skill as a surgeon." Both tall and handsome with dark hair, they could have passed for brothers. "I give you a job and this is how you repay me by trying to ruin my reputation?"

Before they noticed them, Lewis pulled her into an alcove outside a closed janitorial closet door. "This has been brewing for weeks," he whispered. "Let's give them a few minutes to work it out."

"Who are they?" Scarlet whispered back, trying to ignore his close proximity and oh so yummy scent, and the feel of his big, solid, warm body touching hers in so many places.

"The older one is Dr. Alex Rodriguez, the somewhat new head of pediatric neurosurgery," he said quietly, his mouth right next to her ear, his hot breath making it difficult to concentrate. "The other one is his half-brother, Dr. Cade Coleman, a prenatal surgeon."

Scarlet peered around the corner.

"Get your hands off of me," the younger one— Cade—yelled, twisting out of his brother's grasp. "I didn't know it was a secret. What's the big deal? You were cleared of the charges. Nothing sticks to you."

She turned back to Lewis. "What charges?" she asked quietly.

"From what I've heard, Alex was named in a malpractice suit a few years ago after one of his patients died."

A voice she now recognized as Alex's yelled, "What's that supposed to mean?"

"You always come out on the plus side of things," Cade replied. "Something bad happens, things get tough you walk away clean and leave others to deal with the mess."

"So that's what this is about? Me leaving? You still haven't forgiven me?"

Scarlet leaned in toward Lewis and whispered, "I don't think we should be listening to this."

"If we leave now we'll interrupt." Did he have to breathe so hot and heavy with every response? She tried to ignore the warm flush spreading along the right side of her face, down her neck to her chest. "And they'll know we're here."

Alex said, "I couldn't take it anymore, the verbal and physical abuse. You were so young and your dad loved you so much. If I'd had any idea he would turn on you after I left, I would have stayed. I promise you that."

"A lot of good that did me then," Cade said, sounding worn out. "And it means little to me now."

"There's nothing I can do to change what happened other than to apologize. I know it doesn't change anything, but from the bottom of my heart, I'm sorry. For leaving. For everything you had to endure because I wasn't there to protect you or help you."

Scarlet whispered, "How horrible for both of them."

Lewis nodded. "Now you understand why I didn't want to interrupt?"

She nodded. When no one spoke Scarlet peeked around the corner. Both men stood there not looking at each other. Then Alex said, "Can we get past it?" He held out his hand.

Cade looked at it.

Scarlet wanted to scream, "Take it. He's your brother for heaven's sake." Oh how she'd wished for a sibling growing up.

Eventually Cade shook his brother's hand, and Alex took the opportunity to pull him into a hug. "I love you," he said.

Cade didn't reply, but he did pat Alex on the back.

When the men broke apart, they turned and started to walk in her direction. Scarlet ducked back into their hiding spot, sucked in a breath, and tried to blend in with the wall. "They're coming this way."

Lewis jumped to action, moving her into the corner, pressing her back into the wall with the front of his body flush against hers.

Okay. Not a bad plan. She'd be well hidden. But what about—?

Her brain ceased to function when he lifted her chin, lowered his head, and set his soft, moist lips on hers.

Just for show, she rationalized, to create a plausible reason for them to be there. In an effort to up the realism of their fictitious interlude she slid her hands up and clasped her fingers behind his neck.

Just playing her part.

His lips separated and his tongue ventured out to explore the seam of her mouth. Looking for entry? Only one way to know for sure, Scarlet created a slim smidgeon of an opening, purely for investigative purposes to see what he'd do.

And *hello*, Lewis thrust his tongue into her mouth, over and over. Something about the taste made her mouth water, made her body ready, made her want—

He closed his arms around her, deepened the kiss and thrust his hips.

Whoa. Holy hard-on. This was realism run amok. At work.

Scarlet forced her head to the side, breaking the kiss. "We can't."

He released her instantly but didn't move. The sound of their heavy breathing filled the quiet. "I'm sorry," he said. "I guess I got a little carried away."

"You guess?" She placed her hands on his chest and pushed him back, needing air, but not feeling steady enough to move away from the support of the wall.

He looked down at her and ran a thumb along her lower lip. "You look like you've been thoroughly kissed," he said with the small smile of a man re-living the experience in his mind.

"Perfect," she snapped, losing patience. "When I'm on my way to meet up with your daughter.

What were you thinking?" Scarlet took a tissue from the pack in her pocket and tried to wipe away the remnants of their kiss.

"Well at first I was thinking about hiding you and giving us an excuse to be tucked away in our little nook." He reached out to touch her cheek. "But you felt so good. And I've wanted to kiss you for so long."

She swatted his hand away. "We've known each other for all of eight days and every interaction we've had has revolved around your daughter or work. Exactly how long could you possibly have wanted to kiss me?"

"Day three," he answered without hesitation. "In the cafeteria, when you closed your eyes to imagine me in my underwear."

"I was pretending," she lied.

"No you weren't." He grinned.

So sure of himself and his appeal. The haze of arousal cleared. Beneath his respected physician, nice guy, good father façade the fire of his womanizing sex-seeker still burned at his core.

"Waiting five whole days to kiss a woman you've only recently met must have required quite a bit of restraint for someone like you."

"Someone like me?" he asked, raising his eyebrows. Amused.

"Yes." She took out her hairband and started to redo her ponytail. "Someone used to having sex with a woman within hours of meeting her."

He laughed. "If only it were that easy."

It *was* easy. For him. His good looks, charm, and a smooth confidence combined to form a lethal concoction that wreaked havoc on a woman's good sense. On *her* good sense. "You disgust me." She lunged back into the hallway.

"Stop." He said, holding on to her arm. "I'm sorry. I got carried away. But don't go getting all holier-than-thou. You enjoyed my kiss." He leaned in. "Don't try to deny it."

No one was that good a liar.

He let out a breath. "Did I blow any chance of you helping me with one more thing for Jessie?" he asked seriously. "Of us maybe being friends?"

"Of course I will do what I can to help you with Jessie," she said. "She's a good kid and doesn't deserve to suffer for the transgressions of her father."

He smiled, not at all offended by her remark. "Thank you for that," he said.

"I'll defer decision on the friends issue until I see how you do at keeping your lips to yourself when we're together." Because as each day passed with no progress in locating Holly's family, Scarlet became more determined to keep baby Joey out of the hands of strangers and more excited about the idea of raising the tiny girl as her own. And as a single woman it would be hard enough to get approval to foster and hopefully adopt Joey. She couldn't chance rumors of an illicit association with a known hospital player, tarnishing her stellar reputation.

"Deal." He held out his hand.

But she kind of didn't want to touch him since her body was just starting to return to normal.

"Don't be a coward." His smile was all dare.

She shook his hand.

His skin smooth and warm. His grip powerful.

Stop it!

"During our long talk the other night," he said, seeming unaware of how the simple act of him touching her hand affected her. "Jessie told me she's not happy sleeping in the loft."

She'd mentioned that to Scarlet, too. "It has no door. And it's the *guest*room." Jess had shared that it felt like he was keeping her there temporarily until he figured out what to do with her.

"It *was* the guestroom before Jessie came to live with me. I put her up there because the loft has a bed in it."

Made perfect sense.

"But I want her to know she has a permanent place in my home with her very own bedroom and her very own door. I was hoping you'd help me make it happen while she's away. As a surprise for when she comes home."

"I think that's a great idea," Scarlet said.

"If you'd discreetly find out what colors she

likes and what her ideal bedroom would look like, maybe, if you have some time over the weekend, we could go shopping and you could come back to my place and help me put it all together."

"Right," she said with as much sarcasm as she could muster. And to add to her overall 'don't for one minute think I'm going to fall for your scheme' body language, she crossed her arms over her chest, cocked her head and gave him 'the look'. "Like I'm going to go over to your condo when Jessie isn't there." Not. Especially after that kiss. Only an insane woman would do that.

"I'd treat you to lunch." His eyes met hers. "And a nice dinner."

"So I'd feel indebted to you," she said, shaking her head. "Not gonna work."

"I will be the perfect gentleman." He held up his right hand, again, as if that somehow made his words more believable. "Absolutely no kissing. I promise."

"You know I think that holding up your right

hand thing only works in court. And only when
your left hand is resting on a bible."

He smiled.

"And aren't you supposed to be working all
weekend?" she asked. "Isn't that the reason you're
sending Jess on vacation without you?"

He turned away and let out a breath. "Call me
a bad person, a bad parent. But I'm smart enough
to know when I've reached my limit. I need a
break from parenting so bad I lied, to my parents *and* my daughter." His eyes met hers. "I will
not apologize for taking a few much needed days
for myself."

"All parents deserve a break, Lewis," Scarlet
said, touching his arm to let him know she understood.

He covered her hand with his. "Please," he said.
"Will you help me?"

Scarlet was tempted to say she had to work all
weekend.

"Perfect gentleman. I promise," he said. Then

he snapped his fingers. "Let's go to the chapel. I'm sure I can find a bible in there."

Scarlet smiled.

"Say you'll help me." Lewis tilted his head and made an innocent face. "For Jessie, who should not suffer for my transgressions."

And Scarlet understood how he'd so successfully charmed so many women out of their panties. But after the year Jessie had endured, she deserved a beautiful bedroom in her father's house. Scarlet was a grown woman, she could handle him for a few hours. "Fine. Call me after she leaves," Scarlet said. "And we'll set up a time to meet."

"Thank you," he said.

She looked at her watch. "If I don't get back to my unit soon they'll send out a search party." Who would find her alone with a handsome doctor, in a quiet, cozy corridor, with a pair of swollen, red, thoroughly kissed lips.

She smoothed her hair, stepped back and spread her arms wide. "Presentable?"

He looked her up and down. "Perfect." He did the same. "Me?"

Scarlet scanned his person, making sure to spend a little extra time on the most noticeably aroused part of him to enjoy a moment of satisfaction from her role in that arousal. "Button your lab coat."

He did then he bent to pick up his now cold cup of coffee that he must have set down in the corner of their hiding spot at some point.

"I'll pump Jessie for decorating ideas," she said.

With a nod and a wave Lewis turned toward the ER and Scarlet headed in the opposite direction to see if Jessie was still waiting for her in the cafeteria.

Lewis walked back to the emergency department feeling out of sorts. In forty-eight hours he'd be dropping Jessie off at his parents' house up in Westchester County, leaving him with four full nights and three full days to himself. To do whatever he wanted with whoever he wanted. Yet he hadn't made one phone call or sent one text message or one e-mail to any of the two dozen or so women he knew for a fact would jump at the chance to spend time with him—in and out of bed.

Because he wanted to fix up Jessie's room.

Because he wanted to spend time with Scarlet, the woman who'd been occupying his mind way too often of late, the woman he'd just promised to be a perfect gentleman with. What the heck had he been thinking?

That kiss.

He adjusted his scrub pants. In his present state, one size did not fit all.

Okay, so Scarlet Miller had the good looks and trim figure he preferred. But he liked his women easy—emotionally and sexually. Did that make him shallow? Yes. But it also made him honest. With his schedule and work responsibilities, he hadn't been looking for anything long term or challenging. And he had no doubt smart, quick, feisty Scarlet would be a challenge.

Lewis returned the flirty smile of a cute blonde woman he recognized from Respiratory Therapy as she walked toward him on the opposite side of the hallway. He considered a wink, decided against it, but glanced at her fingers anyway. No wedding ring. No engagement ring. It'd be so easy to ask her out, to do all the right things and to say what needed to be said to get her into bed.

He was, after all, a master of seduction.

Yet the idea of slipping into that role, of spouting insincere flattery, and having to tolerate uninspired, unwanted conversation for the sole purpose of getting laid no longer held an appeal. Lord help him, he'd lost his desire to play the game.

He took out his cell phone and pretended to read a message until he passed her by.

Scarlet pushed her way back into his thoughts. Her soft, plump lips. Her scent. Her taste. Her barely audible moan of surrender as she'd softened against him. He may have lost his desire to play the game, but he had not lost his desire for the opposite sex, more specifically, his desire for Scarlet Miller.

He turned the corner, getting closer to the familiar sounds of his busy department, looking forward to immersing himself in his work, of focusing his mind on something other than his daughter's friend and confidante, a woman he could not have.

"Dr. Jackson," one of his more experienced nurses called out when she saw him. "Your timing is excellent. The consult you requested for exam room four is being done as we speak. Dr. Griffin was able to come after all."

Though quiet and a bit gruff with the nursing staff, Dr. John Griffin had an excellent rapport with children and was one of the finest orthopedic surgeons Lewis had ever worked with.

"And two ambulances are on the way," she continued. "Three-year-old male fell from a subway platform. Numerous scrapes and bruises. A notable laceration above his left eyebrow. Alert and responsive."

"What do we have open?" he asked, shifting back into work mode.

"Exam room two, bed three?"

"That works." At the sound of sirens he hastened his pace. "And the second one?"

"Thirteen-month-old female. Possible drowning in the bathtub. Mom is inconsolable, says she got distracted by an important phone call."

More important than her toddler? But Lewis had worked as a pediatrician long enough to know better than to make snap judgments about parents based on limited information. "Do we have a trauma bed available?"

She looked at the white board—which looked more like a red, green, and black board with all the writing it had on it—and said, "Trauma three, bed one."

The electric doors opened. An EMT walked beside a fast-moving stretcher squeezing an ambu bag, manually ventilating his small patient. "Unable to intubate en route," he reported.

"Trauma three, bed one," Lewis told the female EMT pushing the stretcher, and he set his full cup of now cold coffee on the counter at the nurses' station and got back to work.

Two hours later, finished for the day, he took the elevator to the NICU to pick up Jessie.

"Hi, Dad," she greeted him and actually sounded glad to see him. Lewis wanted to run up and hug her and cement the moment in his memory. Luckily rational thought prevailed. "Is it okay if I stick around for a little while? Scarlet asked if I could watch Nikki for a few minutes."

"Sure," Lewis said, setting down his backpack and dropping onto the soft couch. "Who's Nikki?"

The door opened and a little girl with red pigtails, a face full of freckles, wearing a pair of eyeglasses ran to hug Jessie. She really had a way with young children. Watching her, Lewis entertained the first inkling of a hope that maybe she'd follow in his footsteps and become a pediatrician.

"This is Nikki," Jessie said.

"I'm four." Nikki held up four fingers on her right hand.

She looked to be closer to three. "Nice to meet you, Nikki," Lewis said. "I'm Dr. Jackson, Jessie's dad."

"She's a NICU graduate," Jessie explained. "That means she got big enough and healthy enough to go home with her parents."

"And two," Nikki held up two fingers, "big brothers."

A woman with red hair similar to Nikki's joined them. "Would you mind telling Scarlet that Erica Cole is waiting for her in the lounge? I don't mind talking with new parents out here, but I can't handle seeing all the sick babies." She shuddered. "Brings back so many memories."

"Of course." Lewis stood. "Keep an eye on my bag, Jessie." She nodded from where she knelt on the floor, setting out a bunch of dolls.

Lewis entered the darkened, quiet NICU, so unlike his bustling ER, and walked to the first of two nurses' stations. "I'm looking for Scarlet Miller," he said to a young secretary, keeping his voice low. An older nurse he recognized from the cafeteria when he and Scarlet had met to discuss Jessie walked up beside him. "May I ask what for?" the nurse, he looked at her name badge, Linda, asked.

"Erica Cole asked me to relay the message she's waiting for Scarlet in the family lounge," he said.

"She's in with Joey Doe," Linda said with a shake of her head. "If you ask me she is getting way too attached to that baby."

"No one asked you," a younger, nurse said to Linda. "Room forty-two," she said to Lewis. "Come. I'll show you the way."

Lewis followed her. "It's so quiet in here."

"Not always." The nurse smiled. "But we try to maintain a calm, soothing environment as premature infants are hypersensitive to their surroundings." She stopped and pointed. "There she is."

Through the half glass outer wall he saw Scarlet sitting in a rocker beside Joey's incubator, feeding her from a special bottle, staring down

at the tiny baby girl with a loving smile, looking very much like a mother caring for her own
newborn. He walked to the doorway and cleared
his throat to get her attention.

She looked up guiltily.

"How's she doing?" he whispered.

"Still not taking the bottle, but we keep trying." She lifted Joey to her shoulder and rubbed
her back.

"Any news on her family?"

"No," Scarlet answered. "Are you here about
Joey or did something else bring you up?"

"I came to get Jessie and she said you asked
her to watch Nikki."

"Shoot." She glanced up at the clock on the
wall. "I lost track of time."

"Erica Cole asked me to tell you she's here."

Scarlet stood.

"I'll take over," the nurse offered.

"Thank you." She handed Joey into the other
nurse's care. "I changed one wet diaper. She's
taken next to nothing from the bottle." Scarlet

removed a disposable gown, balled it up, and pushed it into a waste bin.

"I have a couple in crisis," Scarlet shared quietly as she exited the room. "Erica Cole is a member of a group I formed for moms of NICU graduates. There are about fifty of them who are willing to come in with their children to talk to new parents who are having difficulty adjusting to the NICU and bonding with their babies." She looked up at him. "It gives new parents whose infants are struggling to survive a little hope. Sometimes it makes all the difference."

"Yes it does," he said from experience. Because Scarlet had given him that little hope that'd made all the difference with Jessie. She was a truly extraordinary woman.

He stood at the desk and watched her through the glass of a small private room as she spoke with a couple. Although he couldn't hear her words, her small smile conveyed understanding and compassion, her gentle touch conveyed support and caring. The couple watched her as she spoke, trust evident in their eyes. The woman started to cry and Scarlet took her into her arms and hugged her while the man turned his head as if trying to hide his emotions.

"Our Scarlet is something special," Linda said, coming to stand beside him. With such a big unit, did she have nothing better to do than hover?

"Yes she is," Lewis said, not taking his eyes off of Scarlet as she handed the woman a box of tissues and led her out of the room.

"She deserves a good man who will appreciate all she has to offer and treat her right."

Linda's tone implied a better man than him.

"No argument there."

But after eighteen years of riding the manic-depressive, passive-aggressive maternal roller coaster of emotions, Lewis had used up his life-time supply of energy earmarked for under-standing, appeasing, and striving to meet the ever-changing expectations of women. He pre-ferred the ups of flirty banter, new acquaintances, and satisfying sex to the downs of compromise, arguments, and frustrating disappointments inherent in long term relationships.

After a childhood spent catering to the whims of a mentally ill mother, Lewis would not regress to allowing another woman any degree of control over his life. Ever.

He was his own man. He did what he wanted when he wanted and didn't have to get approval from or justify his actions to anyone. At least that'd been his pre-Jessie modus operandi.

Now the waters of his life had gotten unrecognizably muddy.

He couldn't bring various women home night after night, not with an impressionable young daughter watching his every move. Most unsettling, with four days of freedom ahead, was the fact he seemed to have lost the anticipatory thrill of the chase, catch, and release. Random, meaningless hookups with generic, unmemorable women no longer appealed to him. But neither did monogamy or marriage. So where did that leave him?

Lewis left the NICU without another word to Linda, entered the lounge to get his backpack, and told Jessie to meet him in his office when she was done. He needed time to think.

It'd taken a near successful suicide attempt for his mother to get his father to lift his head out of his prestigious surgical practice long enough to acknowledge the toxic level of dysfunction in their family. With renewed attention, love and support from her husband and some long-overdue treatment his mom's condition had stabilized.

Unfortunately for Lewis, the damage to his ability to form lasting, trusting, positive relationships with women was done.

Instead of waiting for the elevator, he took the stairs down, needing to burn off some energy.

Supportive evidence of his lack of interpersonal finesse: The past nine months of torture with Jessie.

Although things were finally turning around thanks to Scarlet, his daughter's friend and confidante, a woman who deserved more than a man like him, a woman whose appeal extended beyond good looks. A woman he could not have, who made him want with an intensity he'd never before experienced.

A problem not easily solved.

He exited the stairwell.

One thing was for certain, having her in his condo, with the two of them alone and hot for each other, would only complicate matters. After their kiss, he no longer trusted himself, despite his promise of perfect gentlemanly behavior, which meant he needed to figure out a way to get her help in designing Jessie's new room without her actually stepping foot into his condo.

CHAPTER FIVE

ON THURSDAY MORNING Scarlet fought the urge to fling her arms out to the side and twirl. She tamped down the desire to skip through the halls of the hospital shouting, "I did it!" A manager needed to maintain some degree of decorum. But nothing could wipe the grin from her face as she walked toward the employee changing rooms to wash up and change into a pair of hospital scrubs—her standard work attire.

After months of ups and downs riding the 'I want a baby' 'I don't have time for a baby' teeter-totter, compounded by hours spent obsessing over her finances, living situation, and work schedule, Scarlet had done it. She'd taken action, the first step. True, frequent sex until she got pregnant would have been significantly more enjoyable than page after page of paperwork, but hopefully her early morning meeting with Joey's social worker would lead to the same outcome. Motherhood.

Granted her chances of becoming a foster parent and later adopting Joey would be better if she were part of a married couple, but Joey needed a mom and Scarlet wanted a daughter, and if she didn't try she'd have no chance at all.

Scarlet reached up to push on the door to the changing area at the same time someone from inside must have yanked it open because her hands met air. Forward momentum sent her stumbling into a hard male chest.

How embarrassing. She'd been so preoccupied she'd tried to enter the men's changing area.

Wait a minute. She glanced at the sign on the door: Women Only.

Whew.

"I'm sorry," a male voice said. She looked up to see a man she now recognized as Dr. Alex Rodriguez. "I shouldn't have..." he mumbled, releasing her without looking at her. "I didn't plan to... Damn it." He hurried off.

Scarlet entered cautiously, not sure what she'd find. A beautiful blonde woman, her fashionable attire covered by a white lab coat, sat on a bench, staring at a locker, looking dazed, running two fingers back and forth across her lips.

This was none of Scarlet's business. She walked to her locker and worked the combination lock, already running late.

The woman sniffled and Scarlet couldn't ignore her. "Are you okay?" she asked, walking over to where the woman sat.

The woman must not have noticed Scarlet's presence because she jumped.

"I'm sorry," Scarlet said. "I didn't mean to startle you."

"I shouldn't be in here," the woman said with a sweet southern twang, looking sad.

"It's not like your presence is disturbing anyone." Scarlet scanned the otherwise empty room. "I'm Scarlet Miller." She held out her hand. "I work in the NICU."

The woman looked up and with a small smile

she shook Scarlet's hand. "I'm Layla Woods, new head of pediatrics."

"I've heard about you," Scarlet said.

Layla gasped and brought her hand to her heart. "Already?" She looked about to cry.

"Good things. All good things," Scarlet hurried to add. "From Dr. Donaldson, a neonatologist who works on my unit. He said he was on your interview committee."

Layla seemed to relax.

"He thinks you're perfect for the position."

"I wanted it so badly." Layla's blue eyes locked on hers. "It was supposed to be my chance for a new start. But I had no idea…" She stopped.

"This is about Dr. Rodriguez."

Layla let out a breath. "It's already spread around the hospital. I can't do this." She stood and reached for her purse. "Not again. I have to—"

"Wait." Scarlet stepped in front of her. "I mentioned Dr. Rodriguez because he nearly knocked me to the ground in his hurry to leave the locker room. The *women's* locker room, might I add."

"We had an argument," Layla said quietly, sitting back down. "He followed me in." She touched her lips again. "Five years," she whispered. "And nothing has changed."

This was like piecing together a puzzle on a game show. Scarlet sat down beside Layla. "I've got a few minutes if you want to talk about it," she lied. Because she didn't have a few minutes, she needed to get up to her unit to evaluate two new overnight admissions, a critically ill newborn with congenital diaphragmatic hernia and a struggling little boy born at twenty-nine weeks to a heroine addicted mother, now suffering from neonatal abstinence syndrome.

Luckily her staff, comprised of some of the highest skilled clinicians in the country, functioned competently and independently. And they knew how to reach her if they needed her. "Maybe it'd help me to understand if you started from the beginning."

Layla nodded. "Alex and I used to work together. We had a….thing." She looked away as if embarrassed.

"It happens," Scarlet said. Not to her, but to plenty of her co-workers, working long hours in stressful situations, experiencing instances of wretched loss and sorrow interspersed with jubilant miracles of recovery, men and woman needing to share solace and unadulterated joy in the arms of others who understood the constant demands of the medical profession.

"A little boy died," Layla said. "He was our patient. His parents sued the hospital and Alex." She looked down at the ground. "My name got dragged into the case since I was the one who requested Alex as consult. Our relationship got called into question and now people at this hospital have found out. I can't escape it."

"I'm guessing you both were cleared of any wrongdoing if you and Dr. Rodriguez both made it through the rigorous hiring process here at Angels'."

"Innocence doesn't matter to the gossips,"

Layla insisted. "Being found guilty in the court of public opinion can be just as damaging to one's professional reputation as an actual 'guilty of malpractice' verdict in the courts."

"Not here," Scarlet told her. "The residents of New York City and the surrounding areas trust this hospital and its administration to employ top quality medical personnel. Hundreds of physicians apply for jobs here every year. Only a very small percentage of them make it past the first stage of the interview process."

"But—"

Scarlet didn't let her finish. "People are going to talk. Don't let a bunch of gossipers determine your future. Administration would not have chosen you if you weren't the best person available to head up Pediatrics. If this is your fresh start, if this is the job you want, don't be so quick to give it up."

Layla reached out to take her hand. "Thank you."

They sat there in silence until Layla said, "He

kissed me." She ran her fingers over her bottom lip, again, mindlessly. "We had a bad break." She looked at Scarlet. "How is it possible that one kiss can erase five years apart like they never happened? How can one kiss make me want a man who is totally wrong for me?"

Scarlet had spent the night pondering the exact same thing. "You still care for him."

"I don't want to," Layla said quietly.

Scarlet's cell phone rang. She stood, "I've got to get back to work," and held out her hand. "It was nice to meet you, Dr. Layla Woods." When Layla shook her hand Scarlet added. "On behalf of the NICU staff, welcome to Angel's. We're happy to have you here."

Layla smiled. "Thank you."

Finally up on the NICU Scarlet retrieved her stack of messages and found her charge nurse, Deb, at the rear nurses' station. "I'm here," she said, pulling out a chair to sit beside her. "What can I do?"

"Our transport team is en route to St. Vincent's Hospital to pick up a twenty-six weeker. Estimated return at ten o'clock. Labor and delivery reported a mom at thirty-three weeks with severe pre-eclampsia is on her way to the OR for an emergency C-section. And we have another preterm multiple birth scheduled for eleven o'clock. That's five new admissions and we only have three incubators available."

"Contact discharge planning and find out where they're at with the coordination of home care nursing visits and durable medical equipment for Simms in twenty-two and Berg in twelve," Scarlet said. "We have two more scheduled for discharge today. I'll see what I can do to move things along. Anything else I need to know?"

Deb smiled. "I took care of baby Joey's morning feeding, like you asked, and she took a few sucks on the nipple. She's getting there."

Scarlet's day brightened considerably.

Deb looked around then leaned in and whispered, "Did you do it?"

Scarlet nodded. So far, Deb and the social worker assigned to Joey's case were the only people to know about Scarlet's application to become a foster/adoptive parent.

"She's a lucky little girl," Deb said.

"If things work out, I'll be the lucky one." To finally have a daughter to take care of and love, after all these years of wanting, a chance to be a mom, and she'd help an abandoned infant in the process. God willing, someone had done the same for her daughter.

"What are your chances?" Deb asked.

"They'd be better if there was a Mr. Miller and I didn't work such long hours," Scarlet scanned through her messages to see if any were urgent. "But Joey will likely go home requiring some level of specialized care that I am more than qualified to provide. I put down I'd take a six week maternity leave, like any new mom would get, to stay at home to care for her. So if nothing else, they may give her to me for the six weeks during which time I will figure out a doable work schedule to convince the decision-makers that permanent placement with me is what's in Joey's best interest." Exactly what Holly would have wanted. What Scarlet wanted.

Deb shook her head.

"What?"

"Six weeks," she said quietly. "I don't know how we'll survive without you."

"I've budgeted for an assistant head nurse but never filled the position because up until now I haven't needed to." She looked at Deb pointedly, hoping to relay the message she was the only person Scarlet would accept for the job. "Maybe it's time I started taking applications."

Deb, quick on the uptake as usual, asked, "You think I'm ready?"

More than ready. "Yes. Let's see how things work out with Joey. Promise me you'll think about it."

"Oh I will," Deb said.

With a "Thanks for holding things together until I got here," Scarlet left to say a quick good morning to her precious baby girl, before she got to work.

Hours passed like minutes, but Scarlet found the time to feed and cuddle Joey once and rush down to the cafeteria to meet Jessie for their standing three o'clock cafeteria date.

"Hey," Scarlet said, placing her orange tray down on the table opposite Jessie's. "You all ready for your trip?" She pulled out a chair and sat down.

Jessie picked up her apple and wiped it with a napkin. "Yup."

"You feeling better about the lake and the swimming and boating?" Scarlet felt terrible that she'd missed meeting up with Jess on Tuesday so they hadn't done much girl-talking since their Saturday outing.

Jessie chewed her bite of apple. "Grandpa Richard said everyone on the boat has to wear a life jacket—they keep you afloat if you should wind up in the water—even him and grandma." She took a sip of milk. "And Grandma's going to take the girls to the craft store so he can teach me to swim without interruption."

Scarlet loved how Jessie now spoke excitedly about the trip she'd been dreading for months.

"Grandpa thinks I'm big and strong and smart enough that I should be swimming by myself by the end of the trip."

"That's great."

"Then I won't ever have to be scared of the water again."

Scarlet hoped Grandpa Richard came through as promised.

After another bite of apple Jess turned serious. "Will you do something for me?"

Scarlet swallowed down a spoonful of yogurt. "Of course."

"I'm worried about my dad."

Who Scarlet hadn't seen or heard from since their kiss.

"He's been real quiet. And he hasn't been eating much. I think maybe he's getting sick." She slid a key and a piece of paper across the table. "I'm going to call him every day. But if he doesn't answer I'll need someone to make sure he's okay."

"Jess." Scarlet reached out to touch her hand. "I'm sure your dad will be fine. Maybe he's sad about you leaving."

"He's all I have now," she said. "What if something happens to him while I'm gone?"

Jessie didn't say it but Scarlet heard, "What will happen to me?"

"I promise, if you need me to check on your dad, I will," Scarlet said.

"I wrote down his telephone number so you could call him, too." She shrugged. "If you want. And our address." She pointed to the piece of paper under the key. "I told the man at the desk in our building that you have permission to go right up because you're my friend."

Scarlet smiled. "I'm glad we're friends."

Jessie smiled back. "Me, too."

"I don't want you to worry about your dad. Go on your trip and have fun. I'll call him every day, so if you get busy and forget it's no big deal."

Jessie lunged out of her seat, around the table, and into Scarlet's arms. "Thank you," she said, squeezing Scarlet tight. "I'm going to miss you."

"You're most welcome," Scarlet said, squeezing her back. "You'll only be gone for four days, but I'm going to miss you, too."

In the slightly more than twenty-four hours since Jessie had given her the key to Lewis's condo, Scarlet hadn't spent one second thinking she'd actually have to use it. Well...except for the dream where she'd snuck into his home late at night... under cover of darkness...into his bedroom... into his bed...naked.

Whoa. She shifted her bags and fanned herself, the motion futile in the stuffy elevator taking her up to the twenty-first floor of Lewis's posh upper-east-side building. That'd been a hot one.

But since it had nothing to do with a well-being check, it didn't count.

The elevator pinged its arrival and the doors opened to a décor of opulent elegance that mimicked the lobby. Two antique chairs upholstered in a floral maroon fabric with magnificently carved, dark-stained wooden arms and legs sat at an angle on either side of a small matching table and below a large ornate gold-trimmed mirror. Quiet and the smell of wealth greeted her.

It reminded Scarlet of her youth. The memories were not pleasant ones.

Each door she passed looked the same. Pristine. Just like the bland textured walls that surrounded them.

The hallway, the lobby, the entire building, while lovely, lacked personality. Where were the signs of life, the feeling of warmth and welcome? Scarlet loved her New Jersey apartment, for her crazy boisterous neighbors and the smells of their varied meal menus, as much as its proximity to New York City.

She found Lewis's door and stopped. What if he was in there with someone? What if the reason she and Jessie couldn't reach him was he'd turned off his phone so as not to be disturbed during his four days of debauchery.

"Please, Scarlet. You have to go. What if he's lying on the floor dying and there's no one to help him?" Boy Jessie had a vivid imagination.

She lifted her hand to knock. Stopped.

What if he answered the door partially dressed and reeking of sex? She swallowed down a lump of regret-coated disappointment—which made no sense since they'd only known each other for two weeks and could barely even qualify as friends.

But that kiss.

She shook her head to dislodge the memory. Not that it'd worked any of the other five dozen or so times she'd tried.

Best to just get it done and be gone. With a fortifying breath she knocked.

And waited.

She knocked harder.

Nothing.

She slid her hand into the front pocket of her

jeans, closed her fingers around his key, and prayed she didn't have to use it.

"Lewis," she yelled, knocking even harder. "It's Scarlet. Open up." She pressed her ear to the door to listen for any sounds coming from inside.

Nothing.

Scarlet removed the key from her pocket, and trying to ignore an overwhelming feeling of dread, inserted it into the lock.

Lewis stood under the spray of hot water hoping to wash away his funk. He missed his old life, but it turned out, not as much as he missed Jessie. Talk about a totally unexpected twist. And since he'd dropped her off at his parents' house the night before, he'd spent a large chunk of his 'I'm finally free to do whatever I want' time thinking of her, wondering what she was doing, regretting not going to Lake George, wishing he could be the one to teach his daughter to swim, to help her overcome her fear of the water, bemoaning the missed opportunity to reinforce the tenuous bond that'd formed between them over the past week.

But if he suddenly barged in on her vacation Jessie would know he'd lied about having to work, to get rid of her, exactly as she'd suspected.

Tenuous bond severed.

Served him right for lying in the first place.

More than once he'd picked up the phone to call Scarlet, to fill the quiet. To cheer him up and make him smile. But at some point in their conversation she'd undoubtedly bring up his request that she help him with Jessie's room and look to make arrangements to get together. And even though it'd been three days since he'd changed his mind about having her over, he had yet to tell her. He wasn't ready to put an end to the possibility. And she'd no doubt want to know why—women always wanted to know why, and he had no idea how to answer.

"I want to have sex with you so bad I don't trust myself to be alone with you without a thirteen-year-old chaperone?"

What if the stars aligned and she admitted, "I want you, too." Because after their kiss, he could tell she did.

What then?

They'd pack a lifetime's worth of sex into the next seventy-two hours and it'd be great—Lewis would make sure of it. But she'd want more. They always wanted more, more of his time, his attention, his lifestyle, and money.

Things Lewis was not prepared to give.

And he couldn't risk hurting Scarlet's feelings or making her angry. Not with her close relationship to Jessie which she could easily use to turn his daughter against him. A woman scorned and all.

So what if Scarlet didn't seem the type?

You never could tell. His mother had managed to hide her true self from teachers and neighbors. Lewis wouldn't risk it.

But that didn't stop him from thinking about spending time with her. Doing…anything. He smiled. She could probably make a root canal enjoyable. Pleasurable. He pictured her sitting beside the exam chair, her hand on his bare leg—because he'd chosen to wear shorts that day—caressing him, moving up the sensitive skin of his inner thigh, sliding higher, the feel of her sensual touch obliterating the oral surgeon and the drill.

His body reacted the way it always did when images of him and Scarlet alone together popped into his head.

All the confirmation he needed that calling her to cancel their shopping/decorating date had to be done, and out of fairness to her and her weekend plans, soon.

Lewis turned off the shower, grabbed his towel from the hook and dried himself.

No more putting it off. He set his towel on the counter. He'd call Scarlet now. After the weekend he'd hire a professional decorator. Or he and Jessie could work on the room together, their first father-daughter project.

He opened the door leading to his bedroom, and along with a rush of cool air came a voice that sounded alarmingly similar to Scarlet's. "Please tell me you're alone."

Great. He'd progressed from conjuring up images to actually hearing her. Lunatic.

"And that you're appropriately covered up," she added.

What? He grabbed his towel, wrapped it around his waist and stepped out of the bathroom. Sure enough, Scarlet Miller, star of his nighttime/daytime/all the time fantasies, sat perched on the corner of his bed, fully dressed with her hand covering her eyes.

"What are you doing here?" he asked.

"Are you decent?" she responded.

He stared at her enticing lips as she spoke, noting a hint of shine. Residual lip gloss? Or had she run her plump tongue over those luscious lips while visualizing him in the shower?

"Why are you so quiet?" she asked.

He smiled, crossed his arms over his bare chest, and leaning his shoulder against the doorframe, stared at her. The ponytail she always wore, in the basic hairband she used for work, expensively distressed skintight jeans, open-toed trendy, strappy sandals, enticingly manicured peach-colored toenails, and a sleeveless, silky, peach-colored button-down blouse.

She created a tiny V-opening between her fingers and looked at him. Then she let out an annoyed breath, moved her hand to point toward the bathroom and whispered, "Is there someone else in there?"

Lately she was the only one he wanted in there. "What are you doing here?" he asked again. "In my bedroom? On my bed?" His body liked seeing her there for real and the part of him already hardened with interest from the mere thought of her, got even harder and started to rise up to check things out.

Scarlet eyed his crotch and jumped up like she'd seen a cobra. "Sorry." She backed toward the door to the hallway.

Lewis demonstrated a level of restraint he didn't know he possessed when he stood his ground rather than give in to the powerful urge to stop her.

"Jessie's been trying to call you," she said.

"Dammit." Lewis strode over to his nightstand and flicked on his cellphone. "I turned it off so no one from the hospital would bother me." He scrolled through his messages counting thirteen from Jessie and five from Scarlet. "What's wrong? Did something happen?"

"Newsflash, papa bear," Scarlet said, her calm confidence returned. "Fathers of scared little girls are not allowed the luxury of turning off their cell phones."

He dialed Jessie. She answered on the first ring, like she'd been sitting there waiting for his call, and immediately started to cry.

"Don't cry, honey," he said, feeling like the worst parent ever. "I'm sorry. My phone was off. I thought you'd be so busy having fun you'd forget all about me." And he'd completely failed to consider that maybe she'd want to talk to him about her day or her progress with swimming.

Or that maybe she'd need reassurance or praise or an encouraging word from her father, him, the worst parent ever.

"If something…happens to…you," she said between hiccupping breaths, "where do I go next?"

Next? "Jessie, nothing is going to happen to me."

"That's what my mom thought, too," she cried.

His chest burned in response to her sobs.

"I want to have a say where I go," Jessie said.

Because she was so unhappy with where she'd wound up, so unhappy with him?

"I want to go to Scarlet."

At her mention, he remembered the current topic of their conversation was standing in his bedroom doorway, listening.

Only when he turned to see if Scarlet had overheard Jessie's demand, he saw no sign of her. Relieved, he walked over to close the door. "As much as you like Scarlet," he said quietly. "She's not family." And according to his revised will, on the off chance something did happen to him, Jessie would go to live with his sister.

"She feels like family to me," Jessie insisted. "Please ask her, Dad. Promise me you'll ask her."

Lewis sat down on the bed. "Okay," he agreed. What else could he say to his hysterical daughter who was hours away? "I promise."

After a few moments of silence, in a voice barely louder than a whisper, Jessie shared, "I went out on the boat."

"I'm so proud of you,' Lewis said. Slowly Jessie calmed down and they had a nice conversation. At the end he had to promise to keep his cell phone charged, turned on, and with him at all times, before she'd hang up.

With Jessie taken care of Lewis pulled on a pair of briefs and jeans and left the room to find Scarlet.

"Stop with the guilt trip," she said into her cell phone, her back and shapely butt to him. "I had to do a favor for a friend uptown. It'll take me forever to get down to the South Street Seaport now. You all eat without me. I'll see you next time."

She'd changed her Friday night plans for him and Jessie.

"Right," she said sarcastically. "You have me all figured out. I'm ditching you for a night of wild sex with a hot guy, because it is so like me to do something like that. As a matter of fact he's naked and waiting for me in his bedroom as we speak."

He wasn't, but he could be in two seconds.

She listened to the person on the other end of the call then said, "It hasn't been *that* long."

How long?

"Well," she said. "I'll finally have something to talk about the next time we get together for girls night out, then. That is if he hasn't fallen asleep while I'm wasting quality sex time talking to you."

Quality sex time. Lewis wanted some quality sex time. He *needed* quality sex time. And this

conversation was seriously weakening his resolve
to stay away from Scarlet.

She paused then laughed. "In a closet."

A closet? Okay with him.

"Only if he asks real nice," she said.

Lewis could do real nice.

"I'm always good," she said.

Of that Lewis had no doubt.

She laughed again. The sound filled him with
joy.

"Okay." He heard the smile in her voice. "Tonight I'll be bad."

Oh yeah. He liked the sound of that.

She stiffened.

Idiot. Had he actually said the 'oh yeah' out
loud?

Scarlet turned her head slowly. Their eyes met.
"Gotta go," she said into the phone and ended
the call. "So much for giving me a little privacy
like I gave you when you were on the phone,"
she said to him.

Without conscious thought his feet walked toward her, taking the rest of him with them.

"Whoa." She held up both hands. "Apparently you are under the mistaken impression I am here for more than a wellness check."

"I did hear mention of wild sex with a hot guy," he pointed out. "Thank you for the compliment, by the way."

She stepped back. "Well you obviously didn't listen close enough to the inflection in my tone to detect my sarcasm."

"Let's not waste anymore quality sex time with talking," he half-teased, reaching for her.

"Touch me and lose a finger," she threatened.

He stopped with his hands mid-air, mere inches from her shoulders, and waited.

She looked up at him with those beautiful eyes. "I'm serious."

He smiled. "I know. But I think I need a stronger deterrent because even though you are the absolute last woman I should be lusting after, I want to put my hands on you so bad right now

I'm willing to sacrifice my phalanges to do it."
Actually, he was prepared to sacrifice a lot more.

Scarlet, obviously the smarter of the two of them, turned and walked away. And he let her. "The absolute last woman you should be lusting after?" She moved a used glass from the counter to the sink. "As in you'd rather lust after Hilda from the endoscopy department before you'd lust after me?"

Lewis shivered, and not in a good way. Hilda was big and mean and she had kinky gray hairs sprouting on her chin.

"Or Morgan in Administration?" she went on.

That woman was the skinniest, coldest, stiffest female he had ever met.

"Or Gretchen from Food Service?"

Renowned for her hairnet and tan stretch pants that clung to every single pouch of cellulite as much as for her shiny gold tooth.

Scarlet looked at him from the corners of her eyes. "I'm not sure if I'm relieved or insulted."

Lewis pulled out a stool, sat down and set his

elbows on the island counter in the center of his kitchen. "The absolute last woman as in your friendship with my daughter makes things… complicated."

"Yeah," Scarlet agreed. "That it does." She walked to the side of the island directly opposite him and asked, "What if I wasn't friends with Jess? If you saw me in a bar, would you try to get me to go home with you?"

In a heartbeat. To clarify, "I wouldn't *try* to get you to go home with me. I *would* get you to go home with me."

"Oh you think so?" She laughed. "Rather confident, aren't you?"

When it came to women that would be a capital Y*E*S. To both.

"How would you go about it?" She crossed her arms over her chest. "Give me your best line."

He stood. She looked up at him warily. "It's not so much what I say as how I say it," he explained as he walked toward her. "It'd be loud and crowded in the bar, so I'd have to lean in close like this." He turned her to face him, stepped forward, and leaned in, putting his mouth inches from her ear. She smelled so good. "I'd start off quiet, knowing you can't hear me." He whispered some gibberish.

"What?"

"Exactly." He uncrossed her arms. "So I'd move in closer." He did, brushing the front of his thigh against the front of hers, setting his lips close enough to touch the inner rim of her ear and, making sure to expel a hot rush of breath, as he said, "I forgot my phone number, could I borrow yours?"

She didn't laugh or criticize his corny line. Instead she closed her eyes and tilted her head to the side, ever so slightly, giving him better access.

Success.

He slid his hand up the nape of her neck and, keeping his voice soft and deep, said, "Or maybe I'd say something like, 'I love that blouse.'" He ran a gentle finger down the inside of an arm hole, caressing her delicate skin as he did. "'It'd look perfect draped over the back of the chair in my bedroom.'" Just to introduce the idea of her getting naked in his condo. He made sure his lower lip grazed along her earlobe as he moved away.

"Wow," she said on an exhaled breath. "You're good." She opened her eyes and blinked as if trying to get them back into focus. "On that admission I think I'd better be going." Without further hesitation she turned and moved away.

"No," he said, taking her hand, desperate to keep her close. "Please. Don't go." Because he didn't want to be alone, because he liked spending time with her, because, Lord help him, he craved her with a ferocity capable of significant damage to his manly assets if he didn't do something about it.

"I don't know," she said in that teasing tone of hers. "You promised to be a perfect gentleman around me." She looked down at his hand squeezing hers. "Yet the vibe I'm getting is anything but gentlemanly."

Perceptive.

"I promised not to kiss you again," he clarified, pulling her back to him. "And I won't." He nuzzled in close to her ear and whispered, "Unless you ask me real nice." He'd get *her* to make the first move, to beg him to touch her for real. Then she'd have no basis to be angry with him afterwards.

"Suppose I stay," she asked. "What did you have in mind for us to do that doesn't involve kissing?"

Caressing. Licking. Exploring. "Anything you want."

CHAPTER SIX

ANYTHING YOU WANT.

Yikes! An open invitation like that could get a girl into trouble. Or it could satisfy the increasingly distracting yearning responsible for loss of sleep, poorly-timed bouts of daydreaming, and an on-edge/wound-too-tight feeling that Scarlet felt certain a night of stellar sex would remedy.

"*Anything* I want?"

His lips formed a sexy half-smile. "In the closet or outside of it."

So he'd heard that comment. "We do girls night out once a month," she explained, trying to ignore the effects his close proximity had on her body. "My friends like to share their sexual exploits over pricey cocktails. And let me tell you, I have some adventurous friends."

"Dare I hope birds of a feather flock together?" he asked.

In her case, they did. But she wouldn't tell *him* that. "Anyway," she emphasized, moving along. "Out of all the places they've had sex, and there have been some interesting places, no one in the group has ever done it in a closet."

"I think you should be the first," he said in earnest.

Oh did he?

"I have three that can accommodate us," he added.

She looked up at him. "Us? As in you and me?" She gestured back and forth between them. "As in you and the absolute last woman you should lust after because of my friendship with your daughter?"

"So you have something to talk about the next time you go out with your girlfriends." He stared into her eyes. "It sounded like it's been a while since you had anything…adventurous to contribute."

Eighteen months to be exact. In her defense, they'd been very busy months involving long hours spent at the hospital, with her all female staff. And the majority of men she came in contact with were either married, in the midst of family crisis, or doctors. None of them viable boyfriend material, especially doctors, her professional colleagues, who were as preoccupied by their patients and worked the same insane amount of hours she did. A relationship would never work.

And yet she'd been entertaining some relationship-worthy thoughts about Dr. Lewis Jackson— in a closet.

"You're a standup guy, Dr. Jackson." She used his professional credential to remind her who she was dealing with. "Ready to stuff yourself in a closet for me and all."

"The perfect gentleman in me is willing, able, and ready to assist you in one-upping your friends. And when we're alone, please call me Lewis."

"Will you respond to Lou?"

"Only if it's preceded by 'kiss me.'"

Not gonna happen. After experiencing the good sense eradicating power of his kiss firsthand, and dreaming of it night after night since then, if Scarlet had any hope of keeping things between them platonic, she could not invite, encourage, or in any way appear to welcome another kiss, because if his lips made contact with hers, she would not be able to resist him. And resist him she must.

Scarlet liked Lewis, as a friend. A friend she happened to be crazy attracted to. Would a night of sex squelch that attraction or make it even more difficult to ignore? Would it lead to awkward interactions or ongoing secret hookups behind Jessie's back? Would it remain private or would someone find out?

Would it hurt Jessie or negatively impact Scarlet's chances of adopting Joey?

She refused to risk either.

Time to take back control.

She sidled up to Lewis, pressing her breasts to his chest, reaching up to cup the back of his neck and pull his head down so she could whisper in his ear. "I hope you were serious when you said anything," she whispered. "What I have in mind will involve strength." She caressed his biceps. "And patience. I don't like to be rushed."

"You set the pace," he said, wrapping his arms around her. Two large hands gripped her butt and pulled her bottom half flush with his. "You're in charge."

"That's what I like to hear," she said quietly, keeping her mouth close to his ear. Then she puckered up and made the loudest kissing noise she could.

When Lewis jumped back she said, "Now put on a shirt. We're going shopping."

"Shopping?" he asked, holding his ear.

"You did say anything I wanted." Scarlet walked to the bags she'd dropped at the front door when she'd arrived and bent to retrieve her backpack.

"But shopping wasn't at all what I'd had in mind," he mumbled.

Scarlet looked down so he wouldn't see her smile as she unzipped the front pouch and took out the advertisements she'd printed. "I found the perfect comforter set and accessories for Jessie's room." She carried the pictures back to the kitchen and spread the top few out on the island counter. "I ordered them and they're waiting for us to pick them up at Macy's." She looked over to him. "Of course if you hate them or they're too expensive I can cancel the order. Or I'll pay half. Or all if I have to. I want her room to be amazing." The kind of room a girl would love to spend time in. A room she'd want to invite her friends over to see.

"I can afford to pay for my daughter's bedding, thank you," he groused, reviewing the results of the hours she'd spent on the Internet.

"I thought we could paint one wall this color." She held up the color swatch she'd gotten from the paint store and pointed to the shade with red

X. A dark, grape jelly purple. "Jessie told me you have hardwood floors throughout but this throw rug will offset the deep coloring of the wall perfectly." She pointed to a picture of a colorfully designed rug. "I couldn't find it in stock anywhere local, so we'll have to order it."

"Stop," he said. "The rug is fine, but there will be no purple wall. Not in my condo."

His bland, shades of cream condo. "That's your problem, Lewis," she said, prepared for this battle. "You can't think of it as a wall in *your* home. You need to think of it as a wall in *Jessie's* bedroom. A wall with personality. A wall with posters of her favorite bands." Scarlet hurried over to one of the bags and pulled out the three posters and the lavender and purple picture board she'd purchased. "It won't be a wall of solid purple. We can put the bed on that wall. And hang these. See?" she pointed to the accent colors on the posters and picture board. "Shades of purple. Purple is her favorite color, did you know that?" Scarlet couldn't remember ever being so excited about a decorating project. "She's going to love it."

Lewis scooped up her papers. "You've put a lot of time into this," he noted.

And she'd enjoyed every minute of it. "Growing up I promised myself if I was ever lucky enough to have a daughter, I'd do a better job than my mother did with me." She shrugged. "Not that Jessie is my daughter or anything. But so far she's the closest I've come to the real thing." Hopefully that would change soon.

"Let me guess," Lewis said. "Boring bedroom."

"*Beautiful* bedroom." She emphasized the beautiful. "Very high-end. Designer everything. In floral prints and pastel colors I hated. A showroom that had to be maintained as such on the off chance one of mom's snooty friends happened by to take a peek. No shoes on the carpet. No eating on the bed. No pens or markers. No makeup. No pictures or posters or anything to reflect my style and taste." A fictional set in which she served as a decorative prop to add to the illusion of the happy, successful, fairytale family.

"I like the comforter set," he said, studying one of the advertisements. "And I'm fine with the posters and even the rug." He looked at her. "Jessie can do whatever she wants in her room," he hesitated, "within reason, of course. But there will be no purple wall."

"When I asked about her ideal bedroom, Jessie specifically said it'd have a purple wall. It's what she wants." What would make her feel settled and in her own space. And Scarlet was going to see that she got it.

"It's important for children to know they can't always get what they want."

"Considering her mother is dead and she was forced to leave the only home she'd ever known and all of her friends to live with a man she'd never met and attend a school she hates, I think Jessie has already learned that lesson," Scarlet pointed out.

"She hates her school?" he asked, looking truly puzzled.

"When she talks, don't be so quick to dismiss what she says as complaining or being difficult. Listen to her. She has some valid grievances."

Lewis opened his mouth to say something but Scarlet held up her finger to stop him. "You can discuss them with her when she gets home, *after* you present her fabulously funky new bedroom with the bright purple wall that will show her, and leave no doubt, that you have given her a permanent space of her very own."

"She'll have her very own bedroom with her very own door. She doesn't need a purple wall."

Stubborn. But so was Scarlet. "I am not giving up on this," she said. It was too important. "What do you want?"

"What do you mean what do I want?"

"What do I have to do to get you to agree to the purple wall?"

That got his attention. His lips curved into a slow, sexy, seductive smile. "Let me get this straight," he said. "You'll give me whatever I want to get me to agree to let you paint a wall in Jessie's room purple?"

"I didn't say *whatever* you want, you pervert," she clarified, instantly regretting her impulsive statement. "Like I would actually sleep with you to get you to agree to a paint color. Is that how the women you prefer get you to do what they want? By offering you sex? Paint the wall. Don't paint the wall. Your call. I've done what you asked me to do. You have pictures, store names and confirmation numbers on the advertisements. My work here is done." She turned toward the door.

"A kiss," he called out.

She stopped.

"On the lips. With tongue."

And Jessie would get her purple wall. Scarlet turned to face him. "You honestly expect me to compromise my principles and use my body as a bargaining tool."

He stood there so cocky and confident, attractive, alluring… "Only your mouth."

Seemed a minor deed for a major victory that would mean so much to Jessie. "No other physical contact."

He pulled out a stool and sat down. Then he leaned back, rested his elbows on the island counter behind him and spread his thighs. "I will be a perfect gentleman."

She walked toward him. "For the record, a perfect gentleman wouldn't coerce a woman into kissing him."

He smiled. "Okay, maybe not a perfect gentleman, how about a close-to-perfect gentleman?"

She eyed his naked chest, which was close to perfect indeed. Smooth and muscled with minimal hair. "Maybe you should put on a shirt first," she suggested, because she'd been the one to specify no other physical contact during their kiss, and it would be the ultimate humiliation if she broke her own rule. And her hands wanted to feel him so bad she had some serious concern as to whether she'd be able to stop them. Her palms started to tingle in anticipation. So did her lips.

"Time's running out," he said.

"You have got to be kidding me. I can't believe—"

"Five. Four."

Counting. He was actually counting.

"Three."

She would not be rushed, would not allow herself to be forced into kissing him without some serious mental girding. "Stop."

"Two."

Then again, what harm could a teeny tiny kiss do? She stepped between his thighs.

"One."

She set her lips to his, a gentle touch. He kept his lips relaxed, so full and warm with a hint of mint. And something else, something decadent and desirable, something she wanted more of. She shifted to get a better taste. He opened for her and Scarlet accepted his invitation, sliding her tongue into his mouth—only because it'd been one of his stipulations and not at all because she wanted to.

She moved in closer and, oops, had to steady

herself by placing her hands on his warm, smooth, firm chest. Yum!

More. Her body erupted in a blaze of yearning.

She deepened the kiss, pressed her body to his, and noticed her fingers had found their way into his hair, which was probably a better place for them than option B—unbuttoning her blouse so she could feel his skin against hers.

Her nipples ached for attention. Her long-neglected sex throbbed with need.

Lewis sat completely still, keeping his hands to himself, being a close-to-perfect gentleman. While Scarlet's rational self lobbed idle threats at her aroused self for even considering sliding out of her jeans, straddling his crotch, and rubbing until she found release. *So close.*

"Do it," he whispered against her mouth, as if he could read her mind. "Or tell me what you want. Anything."

Damn him.

So in control, the entire time.

Scarlet gathered every bit of mental and physical strength still at her command. It wasn't much, but it turned out to be enough to push away. Breathing heavy she glanced in his direction. Instead of the cocky expression she expected, he looked as dazed as she felt. Instead of loose limbed confidence he had his hands clamped on the counter behind him with a white-knuckled grip. So he wasn't as in control as he appeared. Good. "There," she said, wiping her mouth, turning away, hoping to hide how much his kiss had affected her. "Now that that's done, let's go buy some paint."

Let's go buy some paint? The only place Lewis wanted to go was to bed to finish what Scarlet had started, to feel the wet heat between her legs, to taste her, there. To arouse her to the point she'd agree to anything. Everything. To indulge in her passion, to indulge his passion.

"Don't look at me like that," she said. "We had a deal."

"A deal that included no other physical contact." Maybe he hadn't minded at the time, it feeling so amazingly good to have her hands on him and all, but he sure minded now, all worked up with no relief in his immediate future. He stood and adjusted his pants to make some much needed room in the groin area.

Scarlet actually blushed. "Sorry about that. I may have gotten a little carried away," she admitted.

Unfortunately, not carried away enough.

Next time. There would most certainly be a next time. And soon, or he'd burst.

In an attempt to distract himself from his body's demands, he picked up the pile of pictures she'd brought with her and sifted through the ones he hadn't yet looked at, amazed at the amount of time she'd obviously put into the task of creating the perfect teenage escape for his daughter. More than bedding and matching accessories, she'd researched page after page of jewelry display thingies, shelves, fancy hooks, and even some contraption called a Bubble Chair that hung from the ceiling.

A lighted makeup mirror. He let that one fall to the counter. Jessie was too young to wear makeup.

A purple lap desk. A funky silver floor lamp. A back-of-the-door mirror.

All in addition to the time she'd spent shopping for posters of Jessie's favorite bands and picking out paint swatches.

He didn't have the heart to tell her he'd changed his mind about her helping him after she'd already put in so much effort. And since the main reason for his change of mind was so they wouldn't be alone together, and here they were, alone together, he may as well accept all she was willing to offer.

Whoa.

He came to a picture of a crib and changing table set. He moved on to the next page, a baby bath, and the next, an infant car seat, followed by an ad for huge pink butterfly wall decals. He held them up to her. "I'm thinking these were intended for someone else?"

Scarlet hurried over and grabbed them from his hand. "They're mine."

So defensive. "Why are you carrying around pictures of baby items?" Please say because you're helping a friend. Please don't be one of those baby-obsessed women who yammer on about their nonsensical biological clock.

"We're wasting time." She carefully folded the papers in half and shoved them into her backpack. "Go get dressed. The paint store closes at seven."

Lewis looked at the clock on the microwave. Five thirty-seven. How long could it possibly take her to answer one simple question?

"I can go myself," she threatened, picking up her pocketbook and reaching for the door knob.

"Hold on," he said. "Give me a minute." He turned and headed toward his bedroom. But this conversation was not over.

At ten o'clock that night Lewis and Scarlet finally returned to his condo. Lewis dropped the cum-

bersome bags of bedding and miscellaneous girlie
junk he'd carried for what seemed like miles as
they'd trudged through at least a dozen stores.

"Having the paint and painting supplies delivered was a good call," he told Scarlet, looking at
where the doorman had neatly arranged the items
to the side of his entryway.

She carefully unloaded their more delicate
purchases, which she'd insisted on carrying. "I
can't believe we got all the shopping done in one
night." She pushed some flyaway hairs away
from her flushed face.

They'd done more shopping in four hours than
Lewis typically did in a month. Heck, in three
months. He should be cranky and exhausted and
looking forward to pouring a beer then pouring
himself into his recliner. And yet he felt energized. Scarlet's enthusiasm for her task, her de-
termination to find the exact item she sought, and
her excitement when she did, made every minute
of their expedition fun.

So what if she was trying to re-create the bedroom of her teenage dreams. Jessie was one lucky girl to be on the receiving end of all Scarlet's creative ideas and planning.

She covered her mouth and yawned. "Sorry," she said. "I was up at six."

Lewis remembered that while he'd moped around in his bathrobe, missing Jessie, bemoaning the loss of the man he was pre-fatherhood, trying to envision his future—a vision Scarlet kept popping up in, she'd put in a full shift at work.

"Would you like a cup of coffee?" he asked.

"That'd be great." She took out her cell phone, walked across his living room, and with her back to him, made a call.

"Hey," she said to someone on the other end of the call. "Can you pick me up at the bus stop later tonight?"

Lewis set the filter in the coffeemaker and measured out enough coffee for four cups.

"No. Thanks anyway. Have fun," she said.

"Problem?" he asked.

"I live six blocks from my bus stop," she said absentmindedly as she scrolled through information on her phone. "It's bad enough I have to navigate Penn Station and ride the bus back to Jersey with the Friday night drunks. I'd rather not have to walk home, alone, in the dark with one of them following me."

She shuddered as if it'd happened before. The thought of Scarlet, hurrying home, in fear, with some intoxicated miscreant in pursuit set off a surge of protectiveness he'd only ever felt for Jessie.

"How did you plan to get home after girls' night out?" he asked.

She looked up from her phone. "I sleep at my friend's apartment downtown, so I don't have to make the trek home late at night."

"If you'd already planned to stay in the city, you can stay here," he blurted out.

She gave him the 'yeah right' look. "Nice try." She pressed the screen on her phone, lifted it to her ear, and turned her back to him, again.

Lewis added water, replaced the carafe, and flipped on the coffeemaker.

Scarlet spoke into her phone. "Hey. It's about a quarter after ten on Friday night. If you get this message in the next few minutes and can give me a ride home from the bus stop tonight, call me back."

Lewis waited for her to end the call and said, "You're being silly. I think I've proven myself a close-to-perfect gentleman. You can sleep in Jessie's room. I'll put fresh sheets on the bed," he held up his right hand, "I give you my word—"

"Stop with the raising the right hand bit," she said. "I thought we talked about that."

"A carryover from Boy Scouts," he admitted. Then, keeping his right hand raised he bent his pinky, held it in place with his thumb to make the scout sign, and recited the oath. "On my honor I will do my best to do my duty to God and my country and to obey the Scout Law; To help other people at all times; To keep myself physically strong, mentally awake, and morally straight."

She smiled and nodded. "Very impressive."

Standing at full attention he added, "On my honor I will not step one foot on the stairway leading up to the loft while you're up there." He decided it best to keep the 'unless you invite me up' part to himself.

She seemed to mull it over. "Then we could prep for painting tonight and get started first thing tomorrow."

"Exactly." Although not his first choice of things to do during their time alone together, that'd work. "I've still got stuff I need to move out of there." Luckily he'd spent part of his afternoon, sorting junk, boxing up his books and journals, and removing the artwork and pictures from the walls.

"I can help with that," she offered.

So far today she'd cancelled plans with her friends to come check on him, only let him treat her to a slice of pizza and a bottle of water for dinner, carried almost as many bags as he had, without one complaint, and now she was offering to help him move boxes and furniture. "Except for your good looks and fantastic figure," which he took a moment to peruse, "you are not at all like the women I used to date."

She gave him a big smile. "Thank you. I'll take that as a compliment."

He'd meant it as one.

"I like my coffee light with one teaspoon of sugar if you have it." She walked to the kitchen. While he poured she said, "If I stay over tonight, and that's still a big if, I need to know you won't tell anyone at work. Or Jessie. Especially Jessie. I don't want anyone to think…"

"There's something going on between us," he finished for her as he placed her mug of coffee within reach.

She pulled out a stool and sat down. "Yeah."

Most women loved to brag about dating him. But he was fast learning Scarlet was not most women.

He held up the scout's sign again and said, "Scout's honor."

She smiled. "How long were you in the Boy Scouts?"

"Through Eagle Scout," he said. The highest, most prestigious level.

"That's quite an accomplishment."

Yes it was.

"But you don't seem the camping, outdoorsy type."

He wasn't, but his father had made Eagle Scout, and Boy Scouts had been the one father son activity his dad had made time for. "I grew up in Northern Westchester. I didn't migrate down to the city until I got accepted at NYU."

She blew on her coffee then took a sip.

With the brief lapse in conversation that followed, Lewis took the opportunity to fulfill his promise to Jessie. "When I spoke to Jessie earlier, she made it clear that if something should happen to me, she'd much rather go to live with you than with my sister. I told her you're not family and it's not your responsibility to take her in. I don't expect you to say yes, so don't feel in any way pressured. But she made me promise to ask you if you'd be willing, so I'm asking." He leaned back against the counter and lifted his coffee mug. There. He'd done what he'd promised to do. Now he waited for the backlash. He took a sip. How dare he put Scarlet in such a difficult position? How dare he expect her to take on the role of parent to a child who wasn't hers? How dare he set her up to be a bad person by saying no when Lewis, Jessie's father, should have been the one to tell her no when she'd first mentioned the idea.

But Scarlet looked up at him with an expression that was anything but angry and said, "If it doesn't cause a problem within your family, I'd love to."

What? "You'd…"

She smiled. "I'd be happy to have Jessie come live with me."

He stood there, speechless.

"She's a great kid, Lewis. Don't look so shocked."

"You'd have to change your life around." Like he had.

"If something's important, you find a way to make it work," she said. "Jessie is important to me. So I'd find a way to make it work. Not that I'll ever have to because you're young and healthy. But if Jessie needs me, I'll be there for her."

As simple as that.

Lewis walked to the counter opposite Scarlet and looked down into her eyes. "Someday you're going to be an exceptional mom to some very lucky children." And an outstanding wife to one extremely lucky man. For the first time in years, the idea of marriage, as in marriage to someone exactly like Scarlet, did not make him feel like he was buried under a ten foot high pile of cinderblocks.

She looked down into her coffee cup and quietly said, "Hopefully sooner rather than later."

Which brought to mind her pictures of baby paraphernalia and Lewis got a heavy feeling in his gut. "Sooner as in that's why you're carrying around pictures of baby furniture and supplies?" Was she already pregnant? Was she trying to get pregnant?

She looked up at him with the same excited expression she'd had when they'd found the purple lava lamp. "Since you've already agreed to keep my sleeping over a secret, can I trust you with one more?"

He nodded, no longer certain he wanted to know.

"I'm in the process of trying to adopt Joey."

CHAPTER SEVEN

LEWIS DIDN'T IMMEDIATELY respond. Understandable. Scarlet took a sip of her coffee and waited for him to process what she'd told him, figuring his reaction would likely be indicative of what she'd face when she shared the news with the rest of her colleagues.

After a minute or two of deep concentration, Lewis carried his mug around the counter, pulled out the stool beside her and sat down, immediately swiveling to look at her. In a low, calm, almost placating tone he said, "A dying mother's final plea for you to take good care of her baby and make sure to find her a good home does not make you responsible to adopt the baby."

"I know that," Scarlet snapped. Her reasons for wanting to adopt Joey had turned into so much more.

"You and Holly clicked. I get it," he said. "You saw your teenage self in her. You see the baby you lost in Joey."

Very perceptive of him, surprising since she'd thought him to be so superficial when it came to women.

"But those memories are clouding your judgment."

"They most certainly are not." She didn't appreciate him talking to her like she was an unstable patient in need of coddling.

"I'm sure you've dealt with thousands of infants through your work at Angel's. Dozens maybe hundreds who were abandoned or taken from their drug addicted mothers. Have you ever considered adopting any of them?"

No, she hadn't.

"I see the answer in your face," he said like he'd caught her trying to hide something. "So why now? What makes Joey so special? Help me to understand."

"You know what?" Scarlet stood. "You don't

have to understand. I'm doing what I want to do, what I think is the right thing to do, for reasons that are important to me." She jabbed her index finger at her chest—a little too hard. Ouch. "Maybe it's the timing, where I happen to be in my life. Maybe it's that I was close enough to Holly to hear her pleas, or that I held Joey in my arms as her mother died, or that my deciding I'd like to have a baby coincided nicely with Joey needing a mother."

"Think about it," Lewis said. "Really think about it. You don't know Holly's family or medical history. What if there's a history of mental illness? Addiction? Or autosomal dominant disease?"

"If Joey exhibits any signs or symptoms, I'll get her the best medical and/or psychological treatment available." Like any good parent would do.

He let out a frustrated breath. "Eighteen years, Scarlet. Do you really want to take responsibility for someone else's daughter for eighteen long, dramatic, exhausting years?"

"Be careful," she cautioned, with a glare. "Your pessimistic view of fatherhood is showing."

"It's not pessimistic," he insisted "It's realistic. And Jessie is my own flesh and blood. Do you honestly think you'll be able to love another woman's baby?"

His thoughtless words slapped the calm right out of her. "I can't believe this," Scarlet yelled. "Not fifteen minutes ago you asked me to consider taking in Jessie if something were to happen to you. Did you not think, that in your absence, I would nurture her and love her and raise her as if she were my very own daughter? Newsflash, Lewis, a woman doesn't have to give birth to a baby to be a loving mother. And the responsibilities of parenthood don't magically disappear when a child turns eighteen." Well, except for her parents they did.

"I know that. I'm sorry," he said. So. Damn. Calm. "I didn't mean to upset you."

Too late. "Well you did. Giving a baby up for adoption, whether willingly or unwillingly, is not an easy thing. On the days I'm convinced my baby lived, I pray she was adopted by a woman who loves her as much as if she were her very own biological child, a woman who makes her feel special and wanted every single day of her life."

Scarlet felt tears start to gather in her eyes. "My personal experience aside, I have to believe that woman exists. With Joey I have the chance to actually be that woman for a baby who needs me, to allow Holly to rest in peace because her daughter will be well cared for, to do for Joey what I pray to God another woman has done for my baby."

Do not cry. Don't you dare cry.

"What do you mean by your personal experience aside?" he asked.

She did not want to talk about this. But the shift from lamenting to loathing worked to keep her tears from falling. "I was adopted as an infant to complete the happy family picture on the annual Miller Christmas card. Their no muss no fuss approach to gaining parenthood status. Mom didn't have to give up her daily cocktails and dad didn't have to deal with mom's less malleable nature when sober. No changes to mom's figure, no disruption to dad's work schedule. The ideal solution. Only they hadn't anticipated the imperfect daughter I turned out to be."

"I'm sorry," he said quietly.

"Don't be. I had everything a girl could wish for—as long as she didn't wish for a mom and/or dad who cared anything for her beyond maintaining appearances." She gave a flippant wave of her hand. "Blah, blah, blah. Poor little rich girl. My childhood could have been a lot worse, and I know it."

"Did you ever try to locate your birth parents?"

Hard to do when her birth was purported to be a home birth and an address that turned out to be in a strip mall was listed as the place of birth on her birth certificate. Knowing her dad's scheming nature, she couldn't even be sure the date of birth listed was correct. So why waste her time? "My purpose for sharing that I was adopted was to show that people become foster parents and adoptive parents for a variety of reasons, some of them self-serving. I can't save every baby born into a bad situation, but I can, and will, do my very best to save Joey."

She picked up her phone and brought up Joey's picture. "She's a real sweetheart, loves to cuddle." She smiled at the memory of holding her before she'd left the hospital that afternoon and the contented little noises she'd made. "When the nurses can't get her to quiet down they come get me. It's like she can sense my presence before I even open the incubator and she stops fussing and waits for me to pick her up. She knows me. She's bonded with me." And Scarlet had bonded right back.

"Can I see?" Lewis asked, motioning to the phone.

Scarlet turned the screen in his direction.

"She's a cutie that's for sure."

"My cutie," Scarlet said. Her soon to be daughter. Oh how she loved the sound of that.

"What about Holly's family?" he asked. The annoying voice of reason. "Or the father's family?"

"I talk with the NICU social worker daily. The police still have not been able to identify Holly. In the meantime, Joey's started to take the bottle, she's gaining weight, and if all continues to go well, Dr. Donaldson plans to discontinue the NG tube on Tuesday or Wednesday. She may be ready for discharge as early as a week after that, and I'm trying my hardest to make sure she'll be able to come home with me."

"So soon? I thought it takes months to adopt a baby."

"Since Joey may still require an apnea monitor and strict intake monitoring to assure she's getting adequate nutrition at home, the social worker is trying to push through approval for me to be her foster parent first. I've already had my personal interview and I have a home visit scheduled for Wednesday morning."

"What about your job?"

Scarlet leaned her hips against the island counter and reached for her mug. "I'll take some time off when she first comes home, like any new mom." She took a sip. "Then I have an old nursing friend lined up to take care of her until she's big enough and healthy enough to start at the hospital daycare. I already have her on the waiting list, just in case."

"Sounds like you have it all figured out," he said, taking her free hand into his. "I hope everything goes the way you want it to."

"It will," Scarlet said. It had to. "I can feel it in my heart." Because Joey had worked her way in there.

"Joey's a lucky little girl to have you looking out for her," Lewis said.

"No" Scarlet squeezed his hand. "I'm the lucky one." She set down her mug as a wave of tiredness crashed over her, making her yawn. She brought her hand up to cover her mouth. "Excuse me."

"You're exhausted. Go get ready for bed," Lewis suggested. "Guest bathroom is over there."

He pointed to a hallway to the right of the kitchen. "I'll run upstairs to make up Jessie's bed for you."

"But I'd hoped—"

"Tomorrow," he said, walking to the front door. He picked up her backpack and her canvas overnight bag and carried them to her. "I'll do what I can do alone tonight."

Considering she was usually in bed before ten and it was fast approaching eleven, going to sleep sounded pretty good. She stood and took her things. "Thank you."

"No," he said. "Thank *you*." He stared down into her eyes. "For giving up your plans with your friends to put Jessie's mind at ease that I was okay, for going shopping with me after you'd worked a full day, and for finding the time to help me with Jessie's room, when you have so much going on."

"You're welcome," she said, appreciating his sincere appreciation. He looked about to kiss her, and since Scarlet knew where that would lead, she stepped around him and went to wash up for bed.

* * *

Scarlet opened her eyes to shadowed darkness and looked over to her clock to check the time. Only it wasn't there. The sheets smelled different. The air felt cool on her face, but the buzz of her old window a/c unit was noticeably absent. She turned to the other side and noted the time. One thirty-seven.

A dim light from the floor below lit the room enough for her to recognize Jessie's loft bedroom.

Her stomach growled.

She should have let Lewis buy her that second slice of pizza. No sense trying to sleep when her body required sustenance, so she threw off the covers, got out of bed, and quietly went in search of food. At the bottom of the stairs she heard a noise to her right and stopped. In the dark she could just make out a person on their hands and knees inside of Lewis's coat closet. With a flashlight.

Doing what?

A cold fear crept up her back, settling into a disturbing chilly tingle at the base of her skull.

Did Lewis keep a safe in there? Was he being robbed? Was she standing three feet from a gun-carrying criminal?

The person moved.

Scarlet swallowed a scream.

She looked down the dark hallway to where Lewis lay in peaceful slumber, totally unaware. She needed to wake him. She needed to get help.

A male grunt from the closet made her jump.

It was a man. He moved again, and oh my God, started a backwards crawl out of the closet.

Doing the first thing that came to mind, Scarlet set her bare foot to the burglar's backside, pushed as hard as she could, shoving him back inside the closet, and slammed the door shut behind him. "Lewis," she screamed as loud as she could over her shoulder. Please don't let him be a heavy sleeper. "Wake up. There's a man in the closet." She pushed her back against the door, straightened her legs for leverage, and used all one hun-

dred twenty-one of her pounds to hold him off.
"You're being robbed," she yelled. "Wake up,
Lewis. Call 911. I need help."

Someone knocked.

From inside the closet.

"Scarlet," a muffled male voice said.

Holy cow. He knew her name.

"Scarlet, it's Lewis," the man in the closet said,
oh so calm.

That's when she noticed he wasn't making any
attempt at escape. "What are you doing in the
closet?" she asked.

"Some crazy woman pushed me in here and
closed the door."

Ah yes, the crazy woman, that would be her,
but better safe than sorry.

"If you're really Lewis," and chances were
good he was since there was no activity in the
vicinity of Lewis's bedroom and she'd yelled loud
enough that if he was in there, he'd have heard
her, "what did we have for dinner?"

"Pizza," he answered correctly.

Alrighty then. Scarlet moved toward the entry-way, felt around until she found the light switch and flipped it on.

The closet doorknob turned and Lewis emerged, squinting against the bright overhead light.

"Well look at that," she said, trying to lighten things up. "Dr. Lewis Jackson coming out of the closet." Dressed in nothing but a pair of skin tight black bike shorts that hugged every curve, every bulge…Oh she would definitely be re-creating this moment over and over for years to come.

"Ha. Ha," he said without humor, probably with some type of scowl on his face, but she was too busy ogling his scantily clad body, from his bare shoulders down, to notice.

He put his hands on his hips. "You like what you see?" he asked.

Oh, yes, very much.

"No need to answer," he said. "Your body's doing it for you."

She looked down at her chest and sure enough, her nipples had transformed into hard little male hormone sensors beneath the thin cotton of her tank. "Don't flatter yourself," she said, crossing her arms so the girls could react to their environment in private. "It's freezing in here." It wasn't, but she ran with that line of reasoning anyway, lowering her eyes to stare at his groin. "Which would explain the, uh," she cleared her throat, "shrinkage."

Then, right before her eyes, his member did the exact opposite of shrink. And suddenly Lewis's condo started to feel rather warm.

It'd been so long since Lewis had had a beautiful, sensual woman so close. Scarlet looked so damn good standing there in her tight little pink tank top and short pink boxer shorts, with her long, smooth legs and shapely curves exposed to him for the first time. He wanted her so much that her eyes focusing in on the part of him that wanted her the most worked as effectively as if she'd put her mouth on him.

She shifted her gaze. "So what were you doing in the closet?" she asked.

"Why are you out of bed?" he countered. Dare he hope she'd been on her way to his bedroom for a little naked companionship?

"I'm sorry," she said, not sounding sorry at all. "Is there some house rule that says overnight guests need to remain in bed until morning?"

"Only when they're in *my* bed."

She fidgeted with a gold outline of a heart dangling from a delicate chain around her neck. And if he wasn't mistaken, her skin took on a slight flushed appearance.

"Well I got hungry," she said. "Now it's your turn. What were you doing in there?" She pointed to the coat closet. "And why were you doing it by flashlight?" Based on her determined expression, she had no intention of letting the topic drop.

So he told her the truth. "With our earlier talk about closet sex I got to thinking. What if you decided you wanted to give it a go? What shape were my closets in? The walk-in in my bedroom was clean and spacious, but I got the feeling that wasn't the experience you were going for."

She shook her head in agreement.

"I had to pile up boxes in my office closet to give us room to move around and paint. Which leaves this." He gestured with both hands.

Scarlet walked to the coat closet and looked inside. "It's not too bad."

"I've spent the last hour working to clean and de-clutter it." And in doing so his bedroom walk-in was no longer as neat or accessible as it'd been two hours earlier. "By flashlight, might I add, so the living room light didn't shine into the loft and disturb you."

"How sweet." She turned to him with a smirk. "The sleeping bag spread out covering the hardwood floor at the bottom is a nice touch."

Doing it in a closet didn't mean they had to be uncomfortable. "I found it in the back and figured it'd be a good idea to air it out."

She leaned in the closet, went down on her knees and reached for something.

An opportunity Lewis couldn't resist. He lifted his bare foot, gently set it on her beautifully rounded right butt cheek, and gave her a little shove.

"Hey," she cried out, falling forward, deeper into the closet, as planned.

He followed her in, dragging the door closed behind him, landing on his knees beside her. "Payback."

She laughed and wiggled around, her leg brushed against his, her foot came dangerously close to—

"Whoa." He grabbed it. "Easy does it. We're in tight quarters here."

She clicked on his flashlight and shined the light on a strip of condoms he'd hidden in the far corner under the sleeping bag. At least he'd *thought* he'd hidden them.

"Once a Boy Scout, always a Boy Scout," he explained. "A good Boy Scout is always prepared."

"On the off chance you might wind up in a

closet with a woman and need a condom," she added sarcastically.

He smiled. "On the off chance I might wind up in the closet with *you* and need a condom."

Scarlet looked at him. He looked at her. Neither spoke. The air around them grew thick with lust or maybe from a buildup of carbon dioxide.

"So here we are," she said, sounding uncharacteristically nervous.

"Yes," he shifted onto his back—because if he sat up his head would disappear into the bottoms of the coats—and bent his legs, setting his feet on the sleeping bag. "Here we are."

She sat squeezed into the back corner, with her knees bent up to her chest and her arms clutched tightly around her shins, facing him. "Lewis, I don't think—"

"Don't think." He reached for her hand and tugged. "Just for tonight, one night, let's not think about anything or anyone. Only us. You and me." His tug progressed to a coaxing pull. "We're the only two people in our little closet world. Nothing exists outside these four walls."

He held his breath. She had to come to him willingly. Would she?

He stayed quiet. He waited. He prayed to the God of Blue Balls.

Mere seconds before he was about to break down and beg, his prayers were answered. Scarlet slid in next to him, lay down on her side and rested her head on his shoulder. The best part of all, she shimmied in so close to his side not even a molecule of dust could squeeze between them.

He curled his arm around her hip.

"Promise me one thing," she said, setting two fingers on his chest, tracing a figure-eight around his nipples, then skimming them down, all the way down, so close, almost there. She cupped him and Lewis nearly came on contact.

He dropped his knees open, as best he could, considering the left one hit the closet door, to give her room to maneuver around unimpeded. "Anything." At this moment in time he would give her any damn thing she wanted to get her to squeeze him and stroke him, to straddle him and take him inside of her hot body.

"Tomorrow." She hesitated, but while she did she kept her hand moving. Up and down. Tip to base. Lower. Amazing.

"Afterwards," she continued. "When Jessie comes home and we return to our regular lives, promise me things won't get weird between us."

The constant motion of her hand made it difficult to think clearly. But Lewis knew one thing for certain. He valued Scarlet's friendship, and would do everything in his power to see that whatever happened between them in the next forty-eight hours didn't interfere with it. "I promise."

As if his reassurance cleared away any lingering doubts, Scarlet pushed herself up and lifted her tank over her head revealing a pair of beautiful, nicely rounded, dark pink-tipped, fantasy-worthy breasts. Those flashlight batteries had better hold out until he had the chance to see every last inch of her.

"Remove your shorts," she said.

Gladly. A lift and a lift, down, off, done.

When he finished she climbed on top of him. "Hey, what about yours?" He palmed the tiny cotton shorts covering her ass and guided her right where he wanted her. The feeling transcendent, better than any other time with any other woman. Ever.

He pushed off with his feet and thrust his pelvis up to grind against her wanting, no, needing more.

"You in a hurry?"

He didn't want to be, but taking it slow would not work, not this first time, not when he was primed and ready. Oh. So. Ready.

"I'll go slow next time." He reached up to cup her shoulder blades and pulled her down, needed to have her hot naked flesh pressed to his, needed to feel her aroused nipples, the curve of her waist, the smoothness of her skin, her hair, her lips.

God help him, her lips.

Time passed in a series of deep, passion-filled kisses and desperate caresses. Lewis felt co-cooned in a place he never wanted to leave. The temperature rose. Their moans grew louder, their movements more urgent.

Then it happened. In the process of rubbing along his erection she shifted at the same time he lifted and the leg opening of her shorts drifted and Lewis entered paradise.

"Condom," she cried out.

Holding perfectly still, when every cell of his body demanded he pull back and thrust into her over and over and over until he finally…finally found the release he'd been craving for so long, was a feat worthy of a gold medal in restraint.

Scarlet eased off of him, reached for something, and handed him a condom. While she rushed to finish undressing in the close confines of their tiny closet, Lewis sheathed himself. When she finished and pushed up onto her knees, Lewis thought, This is it! The moment I've been waiting for and fantasizing about. But instead of climbing onto him, she reached up into the coats and started pushing them to the side to create a space for herself .

Then she closed her hands around the thin metal rod and yanked on it. "Do you think this will hold me?"

It figured. A simple him on bottom her on top wasn't good enough for Scarlet. "So I guess I have my answer," he said with a smile. "Adventurous birds do flock together."

She smiled back. "I thought maybe if you could go up on your knees."

He did. "Given this some thought, have you?"

Her smile widened. "I may have spent a few minutes imagining what I'd like to do with you if we ever wound up in a closet together."

Not just any man, but with him. Lewis liked that.

She lowered her body until she hung in front of him.

Lewis liked that even more.

"Take my legs and wrap them around your waist."

"With pleasure." Lots and lots of pleasure. He lined them up and she crossed her ankles behind him. "You ready?"

"Oh, yeah."

He thrust into her, already knowing how good it'd feel, buried himself as deep as he could possibly go and took a moment to savor the intensity of her tight heat surrounding him, gripping him.

"Hanging from a closet rod here," she reminded him. "Fast would be good."

Lewis gave her what she wanted, what he wanted, driving into her, over and over. Her breasts bobbed at eye level, an inviting treat he couldn't pass up. She cried out when he sucked her nipple into his mouth.

"That feels so good."

Lewis repositioned himself to free up one of his hands so he could caress her elongated torso, starting at her hip, up her ribs, to her other nipple. And while thrusting into her, and lavishing attention on one breast with his mouth, he fondled the other one, because he wanted to make her feel a thousand times better than good.

Scarlet moaned and rocked against him faster and more urgent.

"Faster," she said.

He met her thrust for frantic thrust. His balls tightened. Her body stiffened.

And with a loud crack the cheap peace of crap rod holding Scarlet broke and she started to fall. Lewis grabbed for her, lost his balance, but delayed her descent enough that when they both hit the ground it was on top of a pile of coats.

"Don't stop," she said, pulling him on top of her.

He couldn't straighten his legs and had his head mashed up against his leather jacket. "Are you okay?" Lewis asked, the doctor in him wanting to examine her for injuries.

"I will be in a minute." She wrapped her hand around his erection and guided him back in.

No hysterics. No complaints. A woman focused

on the finish, and Lewis set out to make sure it was a grand finish indeed.

Several hot, sweaty, fantastic minutes later, he and Scarlet both breathing heavy, still joined, she said, "I can't wait for next girls' night out."

He nuzzled up close to her ear. "You're welcome."

She ran her fingernails lightly up and down his back. "Sorry I destroyed your closet."

He wasn't. Not one bit. "You can make it up to me," he offered.

"Oh I can, can I?" She contracted her vaginal muscles and squeezed him. "Supposing I agree to make it up to you." She squeezed him again. "Just how do you propose I go about it?"

She wanted ideas? He had dozens of them. "Let's move to my bed and I'll show you."

CHAPTER EIGHT

ON SATURDAY MORNING Scarlet rushed down the hallway leading to Lewis's condo and used the key Jessie had given her to unlock the door.

Lewis sat at the island counter in the kitchen, wearing nothing but a pair of navy cotton lounge pants, reading the newspaper. So much for getting back before he woke up.

"Sorry I'm late," she said, closing the door behind her.

"How's Joey?" he asked, walking over with his arms out to take the bag and carryout coffees in her hands.

"Joey is sweet and precious as always." She hung her pocket book over the back of a stool. "Another little preemie and her parents, however, are giving my staff a tough time, and I got caught up in it, one of the pitfalls of going in to visit Joey on my days off." She washed her hands and dried them with a towel while Lewis set the table.

"I'm usually the one to run out for breakfast in the morning," he said, removing the lid on one of the coffees to sniff it.

"The French vanilla one is marked with an F." *Men.* She picked up the coffee with a big black F on it and handed it to him. "And I'm perfectly capable of getting our breakfast. We independent girls don't rely on men to feed us." She opened the bag and a heavenly smell wafted into the air. She had worked up a lumberjack of an appetite in the early morning hours. "Spinach, feta, and egg white on a whole wheat wrap for you." She put the wrap on one plate. "Oatmeal and fresh fruit for me." She set both on the other plate.

Lewis pressed in close behind her, placed his hands on her hips, and lowered his mouth to her ear. "Stop," he said quietly. Then he turned her to face him. "You're not late. I'm not in a rush to get started on Jessie's room. And I refuse to let one more minute in your presence pass without a proper good morning."

He set his soft, warm, inspiring lips to hers and all the stress of the last two hours dissipated. Instant relaxation. Except, she turned her head away, "We're out of our little closet world. It's afterwards." Time for things to return to normal, if that was even possible after the night they'd shared, the effects of which still lingered in a delicious little full body hum of supreme satisfaction.

"By my calculation we have twenty-four more hours." He kissed her temple. "To do whatever we want as often as we want." He kissed her cheek. "I don't have to leave to pick up Jessie until tomorrow afternoon." He kissed her lips and the reasons she shouldn't be kissing him started to fade.

All but one. Twenty-four more hours on the receiving end of the tender, considerate, affectionate side of his nature, and Scarlet feared, for her, there'd be no going back to a casual friendship between them.

He deepened the kiss.

So. Good. Arousal started to take over. No. She forced her head away, again, adding a push to his chest. "While you're busy getting yourself all heated up, our breakfast is getting cold."

"Lucky for us I own a microwave."

She twisted away needing some space. "We have a lot to do today." She pulled out a stool and sat down to eat her breakfast.

On a sigh of what she interpreted as disappointment, Lewis did the same.

"So what does your staff say about you showing up on your days off to visit with Joey?" he asked, then took a bite of his wrap.

"They're kind of used to seeing me." She didn't have much of a life outside of work. "If I don't have anything going on, I stop by the hospital over the weekend to catch up on paperwork and check in on my weekend-only staffers."

"But now you're going in specifically to spend time with Joey."

She blew on a spoonful of oatmeal. "Only a few people have commented."

"Like that nurse Linda?"

"Yup." Scarlet smiled. Linda may be a set in her ways nosey gossip, but she was one of the best and most reliable nurses on Scarlet's team and over the years had become a good friend. "She's voiced her concern that I'm getting too attached. If she didn't derive such pleasure from sharing the secrets of others, I would have told her why." She turned to Lewis. "What made you single out Linda?"

"We met the day I visited the NICU. She basically warned me off. I got the feeling she doesn't think I'm good enough for you, which is rather upsetting because I'm a good catch. Women want me."

After seeing and experiencing him in action, she understood why. "Obviously not the right women, or after all the sampling you've done, you'd have found one worthy of an exclusive commitment lasting longer than a month."

Lewis choked on something.

Scarlet patted his back.

His air flow restored, he responded, "Some men," he glanced at her, "perfectly nice, hard-working, decent men just aren't cut out to commit to one woman long term."

"Is that the speech you plan to give Jessie when some jerk of a boyfriend breaks her heart?" Scarlet speared the last strawberry in her fruit bowl and ate it. "Maybe something like, 'Stop crying, honey. He's a great guy. He's just not cut out to commit to one woman long term.'" She looked up at him. "Does that sound as lame to your ears as it does to mine?"

He pushed away his half eaten wrap. "It makes me sick to think about having to have that conversation, of Jessie ever dating someone like me."

His genuine emotion surprised her. "I'm sorry. I was out of line." But saying he wasn't cut out for a long term commitment was crap. If he found the right woman and was willing to put in the time and effort necessary to maintain a relationship, he had a great many qualities that'd make him an excellent boyfriend/fiancé/husband.

"What would *you* say to Jessie?" he asked.

Scarlet swiveled her chair in his direction. "I'd tell her if that loser couldn't see how smart and special she was, if he didn't appreciate all of her wonderful, caring qualities and didn't value her enough to choose her above all the other women out there, then he didn't deserve her."

Lewis stared at her with an odd expression. A little surprise around the eyebrows. A hint of a grimace around the mouth. A definite warmth, with a possible hint of longing, or was it affection, or more likely appreciation, in his eyes. Yes, it had to be appreciation, for her help with Jessie, for providing an outlet for him to relieve nine months of pent up sexual frustration, both of which she hadn't minded at all.

"Eat up, papa bear." Scarlet reached for his plate and slid it back in front of him. "You have a couple of years before you need to worry about it, and we have a lot of work to do today." She stood, cleared her plate, and tossed her garbage in the pullout bin. "I'll meet you in the bedroom." Hold on. That didn't sound right. She turned to look at him over her shoulder. "That would be Jessie's new bedroom." In the interest of self-preservation, she would not be returning to Lewis's bedroom, regardless of Jessie's return date.

Scarlet had changed into a pair of scrub pants she'd borrowed from the hospital and an old black tank she'd had in one of her bags and was on her knees removing one of the two outlet covers on the wall they'd be painting when she sensed Lewis's presence behind her. Already, in such a short time together, her response to him had transformed. Softening. Weakening. Accepting.

And while her rational self knew he was only playing the part of seducer, she was quite effectively and thoroughly being seduced by his sweet words and loving touches. Mind and body. Heart and soul. If she wasn't careful and did not finish up work on Jessie's room and leave his condo soon, she would not escape this weekend without irreparable damage to her willpower where he was concerned…and to her heart.

"So how did a self-professed poor little rich girl get so handy?" he asked.

"I'd hardly call the ability to use a screwdriver handy." She moved on to the next outlet.

Lewis got to work taping at the seam of an abutting wall. "But you have to admit, it's not a skill typical of rich girls."

"I've been on my own since I turned eighteen." Since her birthday when she'd given her parents the ultimatum, 'Tell me the truth about what happened to my daughter or you will never see or hear from me again.' They'd seemed relieved to be rid of her, their stint as parents complete, the disruption to their lives over. "Dad paid my college tuition." Probably to ensure her ability to obtain respectable employment suitable for bragging, as much as financial independence so she'd never darken their doorstep again. "I juggled a couple of jobs and took care of everything else."

She gathered up the outlet covers and screws, carried them to the closet and set them on top of a box. "Not much money left over to pay people to do things for me. So I learned to do them for myself." She picked up the other roll of painter's tape. "And you know what? I found I liked the feeling of accomplishment when I stood back to look at a room I'd painted or a discarded chair I'd cleaned up and reupholstered or a light fixture I'd replaced. And I still do." She carried the stepladder over to the wall so she could work up by the ceiling, positioned it where she wanted it and climbed to the top step.

She'd only applied about six inches of tape when Lewis clamped his hands around her waist. She stopped and tilted her head down. "Care to explain this sudden tactile display?"

He looked up innocently. "I figured if I told you to get down and let me do the ceiling you'd probably go off telling me you're more than capable of standing on top of a ladder and doing it yourself."

"Probably."

"So I'm doing the close-to-perfect gentlemanly next best thing by making sure you don't fall."

She reached up and resumed her work. "You mean you're taking the opportunity to ogle my butt."

"And what a lovely butt it is," he said with a satisfying amount of appreciation in his tone. "But to be fair, it's right in front of my face. Otherwise I'd be much more circumspect about it."

"Cute." She spread another foot or so of tape and needed to climb down to shift the stepladder. Lewis kept his hands on her waist until she reached the floor. Once there she stepped back and held the tape out to him. "If you want to do the ceiling, go right ahead. I'm not some crazed feminist who won't accept a man's help when it's offered."

He smiled. "Upon further consideration I decided I'd rather be in charge of safety while *you* do it."

"Of course you would." She liked this flirty side of him way too much. Rather than argue and banter and have to stare at his naked chest for one minute longer, she climbed back up and finished the job as quick as she could.

When she was done, Lewis moved to tape the other side of the wall. "Jessie mentioned your parents died in a car accident a few years ago."

A topic she had no interest in discussing. "If you don't like working in quiet, maybe you could turn on a radio. I like everything but rap." But she'd happily listen to it to avoid discussing her parents.

"So you don't want to talk about it."

"What's with the sudden interest in my past?" A past she'd worked hard to put behind her and rise above.

"Just making conversation."

"How about those Mets?" she joked. "Beautiful weather we're having, don't you think?"

"Very funny," he said. "I was thinking more along the lines of meaningful conversation. You know, the type friends have when they want to learn more about each other."

None of her other friends pushed her to talk about her parents, and she had no intention of sharing how she'd found out about their accident days after it'd happened, in an FYI type of e-mail from one of the 'cousins' she used to occasionally keep in touch with, the night before the funerals. An afterthought. She slid him a sideways glance. He'd stopped working and stood there staring at her. So serious. "Fine."

She walked over to get the drop cloth to protect the floor. "You want the dirty details, here they are. My parents were both killed in a single car motor vehicle accident. They died instantly, or so I was told. I hadn't talked to them or seen them in years. It didn't affect my life one bit." Except for the sick day she'd taken to attend the double funeral—love and happiness aside, they *had* given her a place to live and provided for her basic necessities. While there, the attorney for the estate had given her the news, "They left everything to dad's brother and mom's sister. You know, to keep it in the *real* family." She ripped open the plastic wrapper with a little more force than necessary. "Which was fine with me since I didn't need or want their money." But it'd served as one last reminder that she didn't belong in their family, in any family.

While it wasn't good form to think poorly of the dead, Lewis couldn't help thinking Scarlet's parents had gotten what they'd deserved. "Wow." He found it difficult to fathom how two people could be so callous toward the daughter they'd made the conscious decision to welcome into their lives. "Hard to believe someone who turned out as good as you was raised by such a heartless couple."

Her stiff posture softened and her smile returned as she tilted her head and said, "Why, thank you."

That smile made his insides feel light and airy. "You are most welcome."

Scarlet went down on her hands and knees and began to tape the edge of the drop cloth to where the wall met the floor molding. After entertaining a brief thought of covering her, easing down her scrub pants and taking her from behind, because damn she had a beautiful body and even after all they'd done last night he still hadn't gotten his fill of her, Lewis forced himself to look away and get back to taping.

"Truth is," she said. "Getting pregnant changed my life."

"I bet it did."

"Not in the way you might think." She spread out more of the plastic sheeting by his feet, working as she spoke. "It made me a better person. Having a baby growing inside of me, while petrifying at the time, taught me to put someone else's needs ahead of my own. It gave me someone to love and hope for a happier future. It made me want to be more mature and responsible."

She tapped his foot and he stepped onto the drop cloth so she could tape it into the corner.

"My baby is the reason I decided to become a nurse. I had some great professors who taught me empathy, caring and compassion."

"Those things can't be taught," Lewis said. "Either you have them or you don't." And Scarlet most certainly had them.

"Then I must have some genetic predisposition." She tilted her head up and shouted. "Thank you birth parents wherever you are."

He couldn't imagine what it must be like to not know the parents responsible for your birth, to not know your heritage. "Your birthparents must have been pretty special people." To have created someone as special as Scarlet.

"Except for the fact they gave away their daughter." She stood. "Oops." She covered her mouth playfully. "Did I say that out loud?"

She sure had.

"My bad," she said.

"Maybe they were trying to do the right thing.

Maybe they gave you up because they thought it was in your best interest to be raised by another family."

She looked over at him. "If something is important, you find a way to make it work. If I was important to them, they should have at least *tried* rather than casting me out as a newborn."

Not everyone was as strong and determined as Scarlet.

"Or a note would have been nice," she said. "To explain why. Maybe a birthday card or a holiday card to let me know they hadn't forgotten about me," she added quietly, looking so sad. Then she shook it off. "Enough about me. How about we dissect your life for a while?"

No. His life was not a topic open for discussion. He felt that same old twinge of anger laden disappointment and resentment that accompanied even the briefest thought of his childhood. "I think I'll go get that radio now," he joked, while seriously considering running to his room to grab the one by his bed.

"I don't think so." Scarlet jabbed a paint roller in his direction. "It's your turn to contribute to our *meaningful conversation*."

Maybe so, but Lewis never shared his past, with anyone. Some memories were better left buried. "It's time to paint," he said. "I need to concentrate or I'll ruin Jessie's purple wall." On the plus side, maybe that'd mean they could re-paint it another, more muted color. Like eggshell.

"Afraid you'll make me feel bad with tales of your perfectly happy, loving childhood?"

Not a chance.

"You won't." She carried over a can of paint. "But unlike you." She sent him a playful glare, at least he took it as playful. "I will respect that you don't want to talk about it and move on."

A woman who didn't push and push until she received the answers she sought was an unusual thing. He watched her, the head of one of the larg-est and most highly regarded NICUs in the na-tion, unconcerned with the flyaway hairs that'd escaped her pony tail, squatting on his floor, with a screwdriver in her hand, prying open a can of paint.

Beautiful. Confident. Smart. Helpful. Caring. Fun. Sexy. Hard-working. Dedicated. There was not one thing he didn't like about Scarlet Miller.

She caught him staring. "You like what you see?" she asked seductively.

Oh yeah. "Very much so."

"Good." She held up the top of the paint can and turned the awful lollipop purple covered side toward him. "I told you it was an amazing shade. Jessie is going to love it."

"I wasn't talking about the paint."

Without comment she turned and bent over to pour the hideous color into a roller pan, not before he'd seen her smile.

Lewis gathered up the rollers and brushes, opened both windows and they started to paint. As time dragged on, his guilt grew. Scarlet had been so open about her difficult past, and when she'd given him the opportunity to reciprocate, he'd changed the topic. And she'd let him.

She deserved more, but where to begin and how much to tell?

He continued to paint. The silence closed in around him. Pressure to share…something started to build until he couldn't stand it any longer. "My mother suffered from undiagnosed bipolar disorder throughout my childhood," he said, concentrating on each thick purple stroke. "Every day I navigated her mood swings like a soldier traversing a deadly minefield. I'd wake up each morning never knowing what to expect."

He bent to get some more paint on the roller. "Would she be manic and energized, exhibiting grandiose expressions of love? Or would she be depressed and short-tempered, impossible to please and blaming me for every little thing?" Unfortunately for him and his sister, she'd tended toward the depression more than the mania. And even though once he'd started to drive, staying away from the house could have easily been arranged, he'd refused to leave his younger sister unprotected.

"I'm assuming she stabilized with treatment or you wouldn't have sent Jessie off with her."

Per usual Scarlet's first concern was Jessie. He liked that. "From what my sister tells me, with medication, for the last fourteen years my mom has been the perfect parent, in-law, and now grandparent to my two nieces. Not that it matters to me because I rarely speak to my mom and dad." He couldn't forget years of neglect when his mom had been too depressed to shop for food or prepare meals or do laundry or clean. Nor could he forgive a dad who'd left at dawn and returned home after they'd all gone to sleep, under the mistaken impression a few twenty dollar bills tossed on the kitchen counter each night made up for his absence, made up for the verbal abuse he wasn't there to stop, for the responsibility of practically raising his sister, of existing on edge, of missing parties with his friends, missing out on his childhood.

Yet he'd accepted their offer to take Jessie away for the weekend out of total desperation.

"What prompted treatment?" she asked.

"Suicide attempt. A cry for help dad could no longer ignore. One that necessitated he stop seeking escape in his work as a surgeon and pay attention to his family for a change." The old rage and resentment started to rise. He inhaled. Exhaled. Would not let it take over.

In his peripheral vision he saw Scarlet stop painting and turn to him. "How terrible."

She didn't know the half of it since, at the young age of seventeen, Lewis had been the one to find her…naked…in a bathtub half-filled with bloody water…both wrists slit. And lying on the white tile floor, covered in his mom's blood was the Boy Scout pocket knife he'd cherished, one of the few gifts his father had given him.

His mother had known when he'd be home from school, an hour before his sister. She'd known his routine, had known he'd go straight to the hall bathroom. She'd planned for Lewis to be the one to find her. And that Lewis could not forgive, because no child should ever…ever have to experience the overwhelming helpless panic…the confused desperation…

Scarlet appeared at his side and placed her hand over his on the handle of the roller, lifting it from where he held it pressed up against the wall. "You don't have to talk about it." With a few adept strokes, she fixed the drippy mess he'd made.

But now that he'd started talking he wanted her to know, to understand. "Living with my mother was…awful." Times one million. He looked down at her. "When Jessie moved in with me, all angry and sulky and difficult, and month after month went by with no improvement in her behavior, it started to feel like history repeating itself. I had no control over my life. Confrontation after confrontation. Trying so hard but never being able to get it right. Never knowing what would set her off. Never knowing what each new day would bring. At the thought of living on that unpredictable rollercoaster again I panicked." To the point he'd actually considered sending Jessie to live with his parents. "But the more I fought to take back control, the worse things got between Jessie and me."

Scarlet set down both rollers, stepped in close and hugged his waist. "I'm sorry. I had no idea." She squeezed him tight. "It will get better," she said confidently.

Lewis wrapped his arms around her shoulders and held her tight, relieved by her confidence, wanting to believe her, needing to believe her.

"And I'll help in any way I can," she added.

She'd already done so much. It calmed him to know he didn't have to go it alone, that he could count on Scarlet to be there for him and Jessie. They stood there in each other's arms, her cheek pressed to his chest, and Lewis had never felt closer to another human being.

"We're quite the screwed up pair," she said.

To him they felt like the perfect pair. But they'd taken a sojourn from real life. Once Jessie came home everything would change.

"You want to know what's even more awful than growing up with your mother?" Scarlet asked, looking up at him, her eyes serious. Apparently that wasn't a question she wanted answered because she continued on without giving him a chance to speak. "That you haven't moved past it, that you continue to fear it and let it impact your relationship with your daughter and women in general."

Lewis opened his mouth to shout out an affronted, "That's not true." But the words wouldn't form, because as humiliating as it was to admit, after more than a decade of avoiding his parents, and in the process, suppressing unwanted destructive emotions he had no desire to re-visit, she was right. Not that he'd let her know. "You think you have me all figured out, don't you?"

"Don't worry," she said with a wink, stepping out of his embrace and picking up her roller. "Your secret's safe with me." She returned to her side of the wall.

Even though he'd much prefer holding Scarlet in his arms for a few more hours, he picked up his roller and resumed painting. "Why do women think they have all the answers?" he asked.

"Why do men think they're too complex for women to figure out?" she countered.

"Touché." Scarlet was not easy. She challenged him. And it turned out he was starting to like being challenged.

"Here's a bit of Scarlet trivia for your inquisitive mind." She stopped painting and looked over at him. "At the insistence of my parents, I trained with the School of American Ballet at Lincoln Center, the official training academy for the New York City Ballet, for seven years and performed in four productions of *The Nutcracker*."

He'd be in awe of that accomplishment later. Right now he couldn't get the image of Scarlet the ballerina out of his head. Her hair pulled back into a tight bun, a pale pink bodysuit hugging her thin frame, graceful arms, strong legs and her chin held high. And toe shoes. Spinning.

"You're imagining me in a leotard, aren't you?" she asked with a smile.

"I am not." What was a leotard anyway?

"You are so easy," she laughed.

And simple as that she'd lifted his mood. Lewis took the opportunity she'd provided to steer the conversation in the more fun, flirty, and sexy direction he preferred. "Yes I am," he walked toward her and turned her to face him. "So easy that all you have to do is blink and you can have me." He stared into her eyes. "Any way you want me."

She blinked.

"That is not fair," she protested. "Blinking is involuntary. I can't stop myself from blinking."

"A blink is a blink," he goaded her.

"Fine," she said, like he knew she would. He had yet to see her back down from a challenge. "I want you up against a wall."

Doable. He slid his thumbs into the elastic waistband of his pants preparing to lower them.

"That wall." She pointed to the one they'd almost finished painting.

He removed his thumbs and studied the wall, weighed his options: Sex with a post coital purple staining on his back, butt and hair vs. no sex and no purple staining. A tough decision.

"Come on, Lewis." She did a little goading of her own. "A promise of any way you want me is a promise of any way you want me."

"I'm thinking."

"Time's up," she said. "And since you worry about me working on top of the stepladder, and all that's left is the top portion of the wall, I'll leave that to you to finish."

They'd completed the painting a lot quicker than he'd anticipated. Now he'd have to think of a way to convince Scarlet to stick around and go out to dinner with him. He wasn't ready to let her go, not when they could have one more night together. "I have a couple of guys coming at four o'clock to help move the furniture down from the loft."

"You don't need me here for that."

"I know we won't be able to position the bed up against the wall or hang anything on it until the paint is completely dry, but don't you want to be here to set the room up? To hang the curtains and put on the new bedding and position the wall hangings on the other walls? Don't you want to make sure the room turns out exactly as you've envisioned it?"

She didn't answer right away.

Good.

He went on, "Then I have a special evening planned, a thank you for your help."

"A simple verbal thank you will suffice. And when did you have time to plan a special evening?" she asked, full of suspicion.

"This morning while you were out."

"You expect me to believe between the hours of eight and ten on a Saturday morning you managed to make special plans for this evening?"

And his friend Clark, who owned a hot new restaurant just off Central Park, had not been at all happy about the early call. But after he stopped complaining about the hour, he'd been happy to accommodate Lewis's request for a table at seven o'clock. "I most certainly did."

"Do tell, then."

"I'll be happy to," he said. "Tonight, in the cab on the way there."

CHAPTER NINE

SCARLET ENTERED LEWIS'S condo after their Saturday night date, glad she'd decided to go. He'd promised her a fantasy evening and he'd delivered, a delicious dinner at an upscale restaurant where they were treated like royalty, a private violin serenade at their hidden table, a romantic dance to the melodic notes from a baby grand piano, a rose from a street vendor. All capped off by a horse drawn carriage ride under the stars in Central Park.

They'd walked hand in hand and whispered secret cravings, shared tender touches and sweet kisses.

"I had a wonderful time tonight," she said.

"The fantasy doesn't have to end yet." An accomplished charmer, he held out his hand palm up in invitation.

Scarlet took it and allowed herself to be led to his bedroom, a decision she'd made while in his arms during the carriage ride. Tomorrow she would return to reality and responsibility. Tonight she'd live out the rest of the fantasy, pretend he cared for her as much as she cared for him, and savor each moment they shared as if it were her last, because come next week, when she, hopefully, brought Joey home, there wouldn't be room in her life for a man for quite a while.

Without turning on the light in his room he turned to her, removed her hairclip, sending her hair falling around her neck and shoulders, and combed his fingers down to her scalp to position her head up and at a slight angle. "Do you have any idea how long I've wanted to do this?"

He crushed his mouth to hers and thrust his tongue between her lips over and over. He varied his kisses, alternating between deep and universe-altering, and gentle and loving. Scarlet's knees felt weak. "Yes," she said against his lips.

He lifted his head allowing maybe an inch of space between them. "Yes, what?" he whispered.

"Whatever you want to do next, my answer is yes."

He chuckled as he worked to unbutton her blouse. "I want to make love to you." His task complete he pushed it off of her shoulders and it dropped to the floor. "Slow." He kissed down the side of her neck while he unclasped her bra. "Passionate." He tugged it down her arms and kissed down her breast. "Unforgettable." He reached her nipple, circled it with his tongue, and drew it into his mouth, sending a spear of overwhelming sensation straight to her womb. "Love." He blew cool air on her wet skin and she trembled.

"Sounds good to me." So good. The fantasy continued. She unbuttoned his shirt, tugged it off, and reached for his belt.

"Maybe you missed the *slow* part." He pulled her into a hug, bare skin to bare skin, so warm and strong.

She grabbed his butt and ground against his growing erection. "Maybe you'd consider a slightly faster version of slow?"

He rocked into her, his breathing a little heavier, a little quicker.

Good.

She reached for his belt again, this time he let her. And while she finished undressing him, he undressed her, and neither went slow.

He led her to the bed. "Tonight I am going to acquaint myself with every inch of your body."

Every inch of her body thought that was a fantastic idea.

He did something to his bedding. "Lie down in the middle," he kept his voice low and deep. "On your back with your arms over your head and your legs spread wide for me."

She loved the dominant side of his nature that emerged in his bedroom. Yet he'd relinquished control in the closet. Once in position Scarlet waited, listening but only hearing quiet, looking but only seeing darkness, feeling the cool air blowing from the central air. Her nipples tightened, her sex throbbed, and her skin tingled with anticipation. When would he come to her? Where would he start? What would he do?

A drawer opened to her left then closed. The mattress dipped as Lewis joined her on the bed. He ran his hands along her body, opening her legs wider, moving her arms so she was spread out like a starfish.

While he didn't slide his tongue over every inch of her body, he got to most of them, saving the best for last she hoped. Yes! He set his mouth where she ached with need, and arousal surged, her hips rocked and swiveled. "That feels so good."

"Slow," he said.

"Sorry, that word isn't registering." She reached down and tried to pull him on top of her. "I need you inside me. Now. Please."

He reached for something, a wrapper tore. He went up on his knees then settled on top of her. So. Good. She bent her knees and hugged him close, felt him at her entrance, teasing in little dips in and out.

As if he knew she was about to belt out a complaint he kissed her and thrust deep. "Yes," she moaned against his lips.

"I love being inside of you."

Love. Not love love, but she'd take it. "I love *having* you inside of me."

He began to move, in and out in slow, even strokes

"You smell so good, *feel* so good." He kissed her again and moved along her cheek to her ear. "So special," he whispered, still thrusting in and out. "So...perfect."

He made her feel more cherished and more loved than all of her past boyfriends combined. Scarlet would never forget this night.

She planted her feet on the bed and raised her hips up to meet him, quickened the pace and he took over. Soon she couldn't talk, couldn't think, could only feel, Lewis's weight pressing her into the bed, his body filling hers, the heat, the intense need, rising, growing, taking over, until he sent them both flying.

The next morning, Scarlet came awake cuddled into Lewis's side, her head resting on his arm, the residual contentment from their repeated love-making leaving her limp. "Mmmmmm." She turned her head to kiss his shoulder. "I could get used to waking up with you all warm and toasty."

He stiffened. "It's over, Scarlet. This can't happen again."

She knew that, they'd both agreed, but, "Wow. When you're done you're done. Good bye, get out, huh?" Like nothing that'd happened between them in the last two days mattered one bit. That hurt. "How about giving me a few minutes to wake up before you toss me from your bed?" Like a mistake that needed to be rectified as soon as possible.

On that unpleasant note, she no longer wanted to remain in his bed after all so she tossed off the covers.

"Wait." He covered her back up. "I'm sorry," he said. "This isn't easy for me."

"Oh, I disagree." She kicked the covers all the way off this time. "Pushing people away is easy." She sat up. "Being an insensitive jerk is easy.

Make me mad and I'll storm off so you won't have to deal with me. Would it have killed you to say something nice? To maybe lie to make me feel good by telling me you had an amazing time this weekend and you're going to miss having me around?"

"I did. I am," he said.

"Right," she snapped. "It means so much to hear you agree to it after I suggest it." Not.

"I'm sorry." He sounded miserable. Good. "I've been lying here for an hour trying to think of the right thing to say."

"Newsflash, Lewis. You just wasted an hour."

"This isn't what I want."

She shifted to face him. "And of course this is all about you, you who pursued me, you who put the moves on me, you who got what you wanted and now can't get rid of me fast enough." She stood.

"It's not like that." He sat up. "I don't want to give you up, but Jessie's my family and she needs my full attention right now. I can't risk her find-

ing out about us and it setting her off and ruin-
ing all the progress we've made in the past two
weeks."

Progress they'd made because of Scarlet's in-
tervention, thank you very much. "I get it," she
said, reaching for her panties and jamming one
leg and then the other into them. "You want me
in your life on your terms. Basically when you
need my advice or help with your daughter." She
found her bra and slipped it on. "Or when you're
so desperate for sex even I'll do, as long as I disappear afterwards so I don't disrupt your family."

She found her blouse and jerked it on. "Because
family comes first and I'm not, nor will I ever be
your family. I get it. I understand." She worked
to button her shirt. "As long as you understand
that by next week I hope to have a family of my
own that I don't want *you* to disrupt. So when you
realize what a mistake you've made by treating
me like one of your bimbo one-night-stands, and
you want to apologize, don't bother, because I'll

be too busy taking care of *my* daughter and worrying about what's best for *my* daughter to care."

"I'm sorry," he said.

He was the king of sorry.

"I never meant to hurt you."

"Those words mean nothing without action to back them up." Scarlet found her pants and yanked them off the back of a chair. "From where I'm standing, you put more effort into screwing me than you did into not hurting me." She grabbed her sandals and stomped out of the room.

Worrying about Lewis coming after her turned out to be wasted brain function, because he didn't. Triple jerk loser.

But just in case he changed his mind, Scarlet rushed to put on her pants, buckle her sandals, and gather up her bags. Without a backward glance she left Lewis's condo, content to never step foot in it again.

Mid-morning on Monday Scarlet received a request to come to the nurses' station to confirm that a bouquet of two dozen red roses and an obscenely large box of chocolates was in fact for her, before her eagerly awaiting staff, who'd congregated like a pack of hungry wolves surrounding a fresh kill, broke into it. She opened the card.

I'm sorry.
L

As if that would make it all better.

"They're mine," she confirmed, tearing off the cellophane wrapper and removing the lid. "Dig in."

While her staff fought each other to pick the perfect sweet treat, Linda plucked the card from Scarlet's hand. "Ooooh. L. How mysterious," she said. "Might that L belong to Dr. Lewis Jackson from the emergency room? What's he sorry for?"

"I'll never tell." Especially not Linda. She turned to get back to work.

"Hey," Linda called out. "What about your flowers?"

"You all can enjoy them, too." Scarlet didn't want Lewis's easy-way-out attempt to appease his guilt.

On Monday afternoon Scarlet ignored the flashing message light on her phone and the stack of pink message slips a secretary had hand delivered to her. Didn't people have any respect for Memorial Day? She sank into the rocker in the peaceful sanctuary of Joey's room, couldn't wait to take her six week maternity leave.

"I've got your baby furniture all picked out," she told Joey who lay contentedly swaddled in her arms. "It's on a thirty day hold. All I have to do is call and they'll deliver it within twenty-four hours." As soon as she received her foster parent approval which she hoped to get soon after her Wednesday home visit.

She jiggled the bottle to get Joey sucking. "I'm thinking a pretty butterfly theme for your room. I may have overdone the pink color scheme a bit, but I've been dreaming of having a little girl for so long. It feels like I've been waiting for you my whole life." Scarlet hugged Joey close. "I can't wait to take you home and have you all to myself."

Someone cleared their throat from the doorway.

Pam, Joey's social worker stood there with a man and woman Scarlet didn't recognize. "I'm sorry." Pam looked truly pained as she said it. "I tried to call you. I left three messages. I couldn't wait any longer."

Scarlet looked at the couple standing with Pam, the woman much shorter than the man, late thirties or early forties, both dressed conservatively, their faces bereaved, their eyes focused in on Joey, and dread squeezed her heart.

She knew what Pam was about to say before she said it.

"This is Michelle and Peter Quinnellen," Pam said quietly. "Holly's parents."

Scarlet's lungs seized. Tiny scraps of the picture perfect future she'd imagined for herself and Joey floated like snowflakes in her peripheral vision. "Are you sure?"

"The police checked and I verified," Pam said almost apologetically. "Michelle is a homemaker and Peter is a businessman in Pennsylvania." Pam made an effort to sound upbeat. "They're active in their church."

Scarlet's mother had been a homemaker, her father had been a businessman, and in their case, active in their church had meant donates a lot of money. Labels said nothing about a person's true character or why Holly had been too scared to tell her parents about her pregnancy.

Scarlet wanted to scream, "Where have you been? Why wouldn't Holly give us your contact information? What was she so scared of? And why are you here for Joey when you weren't there for your own daughter?" But she couldn't speak, couldn't move, felt weighted down and on the verge of complete collapse.

Pam looked down at the floor. "They're here for Joey."

Scarlet's world started to spin out of control.

She gripped the arm of the rocker for stabilization.

Linda showed up in the doorway. "Is everything okay in here?"

No, things were not okay.

Michelle studied Scarlet. "You're the one," she said quietly. "The nurse Pam told us about." She took a tentative step into the room. "The one who was with Holly when she delivered, the one who's taken a personal interest in Joey."

Much more than a personal interest, she loved the baby sleeping in her arms, she'd hoped and planned and dreamed… The heaviness of loss and despair settled on her chest.

"Did Holly…?" Michelle brought a tissue up to her nose. "Did Holly suffer?" She let out a sob and Peter put his arm around his wife and tucked her into the side of his taller body, strong and protective.

Scarlet gave the woman points for believable concern for her daughter and the man points for believable concern for his wife. She pushed her

personal hurt aside, gathered up some profession-
alism and answered, "It was quick. She didn't
suffer." Even if she had, what would be the point
of telling the girl's parents?

"Thank you for being there with her," Michelle
said, looking like she was barely holding it together. Scarlet knew the feeling. "And for taking
such good care of baby Joey."

Scarlet didn't want a thank you. She wanted
to stand up and run and take Joey with her. She
wanted to cuddle and love and raise Joey, she
wanted them to be a family. They were supposed
to be a family.

But Joey had her own family, one that did not
include Scarlet.

"May I hold her?" Michelle asked.

No you may not!

"Holly begged me to find Joey a good home
with a nice family," Scarlet said. "If you'd answer
me one question, I need to understand why she
didn't think that good home with a nice family
was with your family?"

254 NYC ANGELS: TEMPTING NURSE SCARLET

"We taught our daughter abstinence," Peter finally spoke. "We live in a small community. The members of our church, who comprise the majority of our closest friends, would not have looked kindly on Holly's pregnancy."

"We didn't even know she had a boyfriend," Michelle said. "But she's our daughter, our blessing, our only child. We loved her, unconditionally. Nothing would ever have changed that. Nothing," she said firmly. "She should have come to us, I wish she'd come to us. We would have understood, we would have helped her and protected her."

"That's the truth," Peter said.

"Then maybe she'd still be here." Michelle's voice cracked. "Why did she trust that woman more than her own mother?" She looked up at Peter and started to cry. "Why?"

"We'll never know," Peter said, taking his wife into his arms, trying to fight his own tears. "You need to be strong for little Joey." He rubbed Michelle's back. "She needs us to be strong."

"What woman?" Scarlet asked.

"Holly ran away thirty-four days ago," Michelle said, sounding heartbroken. "We have been looking for her around the clock since then. We never considered she'd come all the way to New York City by herself."

Pam entered the conversation. "The police made the connection during a raid on a brownstone on the lower east side, suspected baby brokers who made contact with pregnant teens online. During a search they found Holly's wallet in a box."

"May I hold her?" Michelle asked again, taking another step closer.

Scarlet stared down at Joey, fast asleep, the baby's tiny hand holding onto her index finger, totally unaware of the tumultuous feelings churning inside of Scarlet as she prepared to give up yet another daughter. So what if she hadn't yet been approved and the paperwork hadn't yet been signed. In Scarlet's heart, Joey was hers.

"Come," Linda said. "You need to wash your

hands and put on disposable gowns. Do either of you have any signs of cold or illness?"

With the Quinnellens occupied, Pam walked over to Scarlet. "I'm so sorry," she whispered. "I know how much—"

"Don't," Scarlet snapped. "Not here. Not now."

Pam placed a sympathetic hand on Scarlet's shoulder and nodded in understanding.

Transferring Joey into Michelle's arms was the absolute hardest thing Scarlet had ever done. A slight joy when Joey cried out her dissatisfaction at being taken from Scarlet, because she recognized Scarlet and preferred her to all others, was quickly tamped down by Scarlet's professional responsibility to ease the transition which was in Joey's best interest.

"She likes it when you tilt her like this." At the sound of her voice, Joey went silent. Scarlet repositioned Joey to face into Michelle more. She moved away and Joey started to cry again. Michelle looked stricken. So Scarlet went down on her knees and moved in close to both grandmother and baby. "Come on, you grumpy girl. Take the bottle for your grandma."

Michelle put the nipple into Joey's mouth and the baby started to suck.

"That's a good girl." She leaned forward and placed a kiss on Joey's forehead. "Good bye, sweet baby," she whispered for only Joey to hear, the ache of loss tearing at her heart, a throbbing pressure building in her head as each bubble of hope she'd had for her and Joey's future together burst then vanished.

When Scarlet tried to stand up, praying her legs would hold her, Michelle pulled her into a one-armed hug. "Thank you," she said. "I can see how much you love baby Joey and I want to assure you we will do right by this little girl. And we'll make sure she never forgets the special nurse who took such loving good care of her and watched over her until we could find her. We'll make sure she knows she can talk to us about anything and we will always love her and be there for her, no matter what."

Scarlet couldn't hold back her tears. "Thank you for that." But she'd reached her limit, had to leave this room this instant. With her last bit of strength she stood and wiped her eyes. "I, uh…" Despair clogged her throat at the thought of leaving Joey. She cleared it, had to be strong. "…have to get back to work. Linda would you familiarize Mr. and Mrs. Quinnellen with Joey's medical status, care to date, and her treatment/discharge plan."

"Of course," Linda said quietly. "Don't you worry about a thing."

When Scarlet left the room she came face to face with many sad, concerned faces as the majority of her day shift staff stared back at her from behind the nurses' station. Thank goodness her charge nurse, Deb, was among them. "Back to work everyone," Scarlet said. "I need to speak to you in my office, Deb."

As soon as Deb followed her in and closed the door Scarlet said, "I need to head out." Her voice cracked, and Scarlet hoped she'd be able to hold herself together long enough to make it out of the hospital.

"I'm so sorry," Deb said.

Scarlet couldn't talk about it. "You're in charge," she told Deb, discarding her gown. "And I am entrusting you with the task of making sure Joey's grandparents are trained and proficient in all the care she'll require on discharge." A clean break would make it easier for everyone involved, which meant she'd just held and cuddled and kissed Joey for the last time. Tears burned her eyes. She kept her head down and pulled open the bottom drawer of her desk to retrieve her pocketbook. "If you have any concerns let me know."

"Of course," Deb said.

Someone knocked on her door.

Scarlet didn't look up. "Who is it?" she asked Deb.

"Pam and a woman I've never seen before," Deb said quietly.

"Seconds from a clean getaway," Scarlet whispered.

"What should I do?" Deb asked.

Scarlet didn't feel capable of pretending she was okay. But Pam knew how much she wanted Joey and how devastating the surprise arrival of her grandparents had been. If she were knocking on Scarlet's door it must be important, so she looked up and motioned for them enter.

"This is Polly Seymour," Pam said from the doorway. "A family friend of the Quinnellens."

"I'm a nurse and I've dreamed of working here at Angel's," Polly said way too enthusiastically for the mood in the office as she reached out to shake Scarlet's hand.

Scarlet shot a why-did-you-bring-this-woman-into-my-office look at Pam who immediately responded, "She accompanied Michelle and Peter to New York in case they needed assistance with Joey's care. I thought she could put your mind at ease about the type of people they are."

Was the concern in Pam's eyes for Scarlet or for Joey?

"They're lovely," Polly said. "Truly lovely people. We've attended the same church for years. I'd have given anything for a mother, who am I kidding, for any member of my family to be as attentive and caring as Michelle." Although Scarlet didn't know the woman, she had an impassioned sincerity in her tone that made her words believable. "Peter may look strict and in charge, but Michelle calls the shots in that family."

Scarlet got the feeling that was a good thing.

Polly chattered on about a county fair and an angry uncle and Michelle coming to her aid. But it was more information than Scarlet could handle in her present frame of mind. She glanced at Deb for help.

"Thank you so much for stopping by," Deb stood, interrupting Polly mid-perky sentence. "If Scarlet doesn't leave now she'll be late for an important meeting."

"Oh, of course," Polly said. "We can't have that now, can we?"

Deb herded Polly and Pam toward the door.

"While I'm here I'm going to apply for a job," Polly said, over her shoulder.

"Best of luck," Deb said, closing the door behind them.

"Thank you," Scarlet said.

"Why don't you head over to my place? Kev is working from home today and I'll get there as soon as I can. You shouldn't be alone."

"I'll be fine," she said with a forced smile. "I'll have my cell phone on for emergencies."

"Well turn it off and focus on you for a change," Deb said. "Tonight *I'll* have *my* cell phone on and I'm going to leave word that I'm on call for emergencies. You go home and take care of you."

Scarlet picked up her phone to turn it off. Joey's picture came up and Scarlet could take no more. She set her head down on the desk and started to cry. And what made the entire situation infinitely worse was the one person she wanted to

run to and confide in and accept comfort from—
Lewis—had unceremoniously kicked her out of
his life.

And now she'd lost Joey, too.

Scarlet had never felt more alone.

Deb pulled up a chair, sat down beside her and
rubbed Scarlet's back. "Get it all out."

Scarlet worried if she didn't get this mini-
outburst under control she'd be there all night.
She sniffled and grabbed for a tissue.

"When you're done," Deb continued, "we'll
head down to the cafeteria for some hot fudge
sundaes."

Scarlet laughed then sat up and wiped her eyes.
"I will not be responsible for you cheating on
your diet."

"Fine," Deb said with a pout. "Then I'll sit there
and watch *you* eat one."

"Only a true friend would do that," Scarlet said,
squeezing Deb's arm. "But it's not necessary."
The laugh made her feel a little better so she took

the opportunity to make her exit. "Will you run interference for me?"

"Sure thing your head nurseness." Deb stood and bowed. "Call me if you need me."

"I will." No she wouldn't.

Lewis followed the GPS directions to Scarlet's three story, Robin's egg blue apartment building then drove around the residential block in search of street parking, losing patience, anxious to see her and be with her. The smell of sausage and peppers greeted him as he entered her building. A child's or children's crayon drawings taped along the walls welcomed him. Each of the four doors on the first floor was painted a different color, each with its own unique decorations.

He climbed the worn wooden stairs to the second floor and stopped at the bright turquoise door with the big red Welcome sign and the small plate of wrapped chocolates hanging from an interesting wire rack, lucky number seven. Scarlet's apartment.

So warm and inviting. So Scarlet.

He knocked.

No answer.

He imagined her inside, heartbroken and distraught, and knocked even harder. "Scarlet," he yelled. "It's Lewis, open up."

He gave her a couple of minutes but still no answer.

He pounded with the side of his fist. "I know you're in there." Actually, he didn't. "I'm not leaving until you open this door." Because he didn't know where else to look for her, but he'd beat on every door in this building if he had to. He would not leave until he found her.

The door opened about three inches. "There. I opened it. Now leave." She started to close it.

He jammed his hand in so she couldn't, but that didn't stop her from trying. Ouch! "Wait."

"I'm feeling sorry for myself," she said, sounding weary. "It's not pretty. Go away."

Pretty or not he had no intention of leaving her alone and miserable. He pushed on the door. "Let me in."

She pushed back. "No. Shouldn't you be on your way to get Jessie?"

"When I heard about Joey's grandparents showing up I called my dad and told him I had to take care of something important." *Someone* important. "He and mom offered to bring Jessie into the city after dinner." Which they were more than happy to do for the chance to see the inside of his condo for the first time.

"Great. Poor pitiful Scarlet got too attached to one of her patients. News of my breakdown is probably all over the hospital by now." She must have walked away because all of a sudden the door flew open and Lewis, who had his shoulder pressed against it, lurched forward into her apartment with its tiny sunny yellow kitchen and eclectic mix of old and modern furniture.

He walked to where she'd plopped onto the couch and wrapped herself in a colorfully striped afghan, noting all the crumpled tissues on the coffee table and floor.

"Joey was more than a patient," he acknowledged. "And I have no idea what's circulating around the hospital." He moved to the far end of the couch and sat down. "Your nurse Linda called the ER and insisted they get in touch with me immediately."

"Linda can be pretty insistent," Scarlet said.

More like relentless. To the point she'd harassed the unit secretary to tears. "I called her back and she told me what happened." At which time Lewis's heart had stopped. "She gave me your address." And told him if he wanted to prove himself worthy of Scarlet, this was his chance.

Without any further thought of his mother, or his avoidance of long term relationships with women, or how a relationship with Scarlet might affect Jessie, Lewis had grabbed his car keys and left his condo. Scarlet needed him and worthy or not, he would be there for her.

After a solid twenty-four hours considering his life, past, present, and future, and Jessie's life, past, present, and future, Lewis came the decision he could not, would not, give up Scarlet.

She'd become an integral part, a special part, of his life. He could love her, he would love her. He felt certain of it.

Somewhere in the Lincoln Tunnel Lewis decided he *did* want to prove himself worthy of Scarlet, he wanted to be the type of man she deserved, the type of man she'd want to spend her time with, her life with. By going to her, putting her before Jessie, and demonstrating with his actions how much he cared, Lewis hoped to be taking the first steps toward convincing her.

Scarlet smoothed down her messy hair. "Sorry she bothered you."

"I'm not sorry, and it wasn't a bother." He *wanted* to be the one to comfort her and take care of her, to show her how much she meant to him. "How are you doing?" A stupid question he regretted the second it left his mouth. If her puffy red eyes and her pink nose and dry lips were any indication, she'd probably been crying for hours.

"How do you think I'm doing?" she asked

calmly. "Today I lost my second daughter. Today it became clear I am destined to spend the rest of my life taking care of other peoples' babies, never to have one of my own, to live alone and be alone." She grabbed a tissue from the box beside her and blotted at her eyes.

"You're not alone," he said, reaching for her hand which she moved away.

She looked up at him with red puffy eyes. "No. At this particular moment in time I am not alone. But in two minutes when you leave here to meet up with your parents and your daughter I'll be alone, and the night after that and the night after that and the night after that." She started to cry and Lewis's entire body ached to hold her.

"Come home with me," he offered. "Come be there when Jessie sees her new room for the first time." *Let me take care of you.* "It'll cheer you up."

"Jessie's *your* daughter," she said. "I don't belong there."

"Of course you do." He slid closer intending to

put his arm around her and tell her how important she was to both him and Jessie.

But she pushed him away. "Don't," she snapped. "Don't think you can come in here pretending to care about me," she yelled. "You don't get to turn it on and turn it off when it suits you. It's over," she screamed. "This can't happen again." She threw his callous words back in his face.

"I didn't mean—"

"Yes you did," she sobbed. "I can't handle this right now. I need you to leave."

"But I want—"

"Don't you get it?" she yelled. "I'm done caring about what you want. You used me—"

"I did not."

She glared at him. "You hurt me, and having you here is making me feel worse, not better. Now get out," she screamed wildly, throwing off the afghan and stomping to the door which she yanked open. "Get. Out." Tears streamed down her cheeks.

Lewis stood. "Let me make you a cup of tea."

To calm her down so they could talk, so he could fix things between them.

"I don't want tea," she screamed. "And I don't want you, in my apartment or anywhere near me."

Her words slammed into his diaphragm, inhibiting his ability to draw in the air necessary to make speech possible.

"Please go," she said, leaning her back against the door, looking exhausted and completely defeated. "You shouldn't have come."

Lewis didn't agree, but rather than upset her further, he left.

CHAPTER TEN

ABOUT HALF PAST six the following Monday evening Scarlet sat in her office reviewing Joey's chart, especially Deb's notes regarding discharge readiness. Joey thrived under Michelle's constant attention and was scheduled to go home tomorrow. In the past week Scarlet had managed to put aside her sorrow enough to be happy for Joey, and for Michelle and Peter. They'd fallen in love with Joey as quickly as Scarlet had, and she felt at peace with Joey going home with her family where she belonged.

Michelle promised to send pictures, which Scarlet would proudly hang up on the wall with all the other NICU graduates.

One of the unit secretaries came to her door. "I know you said you didn't want to be bothered unless it was an emergency, but there's a girl on the phone for you. She says her name is Jessie and she sounds upset."

"Put her through," Scarlet said and disengaged her Do Not Disturb button so she could answer the call. Come on. Come on. Had something happened to Jess? To Lewis? She tapped her pen on her desk blotter while she waited.

As soon as the phone rang Scarlet snatched up the receiver. "Hey, Jess. What's wrong?"

"I got it," Jess said.

"You got what?"

"*It*," she said with emphasis. "I need stuff."

"What language are you speaking, because I'm not following."

"The cramping crimson curse."

For the first time in days Scarlet smiled. "So if I'm deciphering this correctly, you got your period and are in need of some feminine supplies. Welcome to womanhood."

"Please don't talk like that. It makes me want to vomit."

Scarlet's smile grew. "Where are you?"

"In the bathroom."

"Where's your dad?"

"Outside of the bathroom yelling that dinner will be ready in fifteen minutes. How soon can you get here?"

The last place Scarlet wanted to go was to Lewis's condo, to be reminded of what they'd shared. "You know you can talk to your dad," she said. "I'm sure he'd—"

"Do not go there," Jessie interrupted. "You told me if I ever needed you, and I need you."

Truth be told, the place she wanted to go even less than Lewis's condo was back to her apartment and the empty bedroom with pink walls and butterfly decals that'd been waiting for Joey—which is why she'd been putting off leaving the hospital tonight. Jessie needing her gave Scarlet an excuse to put it off for a little while longer. "I'll swing by the drugstore, and assuming I can catch a cab, I'll be there in twenty minutes."

"Thank you," Jessie said and disconnected the call.

Half an hour later Scarlet exited the elevator

on Lewis's floor and tried to ignore the memory of them walking down this very corridor, hand in hand, so happy.

She reached his door and knocked.

Expecting Jessie to answer, she felt as shocked as Lewis looked when he opened the door.

"What are you doing here?" he asked softly.

"I'm sorry to bother you," she said, holding up the drugstore bag. "Jessie called me."

"Scarlet," he said, his voice filled with emotion. "You could never bother me. You're welcome here anytime."

Yet he didn't open the door enough to allow entry. "May I come in?"

"Yes. Of course." He moved to the side and opened the door wider. "Please. Come in."

Jessie stood in the living room.

"I got what you—"

"I lied," Jessie said. "I didn't…you know." She walked over to Scarlet and took the bag from her hand. "But when I do, now I'll be ready."

"Why?" Scarlet asked.

Jessie moved to close the door to the hallway then she positioned herself in front of it as if trying to block Scarlet's exit. "Because you two need to talk."

"Jessie," Lewis cautioned.

"I know. It was wrong, and I'm sorry." She glanced back and forth between them before stopping on Scarlet. "Dad told me you both spent a lot of time together working on my room."

Among other things. Hopefully the warmth on her face did not present itself as the bright red blush she feared.

"He really likes you as in more than a friend likes you," Jessie said.

"That was supposed to be a private father daughter conversation," Lewis interjected.

He'd told Jessie he really liked her?

Undeterred by Lewis's scowl Jessie continued, "He wanted to know how I'd feel if he asked you out on a date."

"That's enough," Lewis said.

No it wasn't, not until Scarlet heard her answer. "What did you tell him?"

Jessie rested her back against the door and clasped her fingers together over her belly. "Before my mom died, we spent a lot of time talking. She said she had to cram years of motherly wisdom and advice into a few short weeks so I'd better be prepared to listen." Jessie's lips curved into a small smile at the memory. "I am totally covered on *it*," she locked eyes with Scarlet, "dating and safe sex. So neither of you need to worry."

Yeah right.

"She also told me that she'd always be my mom and no one could replace her in my heart. But that didn't mean I shouldn't make room in my heart for another mom someday, because there was plenty of room in there, and she didn't mind sharing."

Tears welled in Scarlet's eyes. "I think I would have liked your mom."

"I *know* she would have liked you," Jessie said with tears in her eyes, too.

"We talked about this, honey," Lewis said to Jess. "Scarlet and I dating does not mean we're going to get married."

Of course it didn't, because to men like Lewis, dating equaled sex and marriage didn't fit into the equation.

"I know that," Jessie said, wiping at the corner of her eye. "Mom dated lots of guys. To be honest," she looked up at Lewis, "I kind of wondered if you even liked women anymore since you haven't gone on a date for the whole nine months I've been living here."

Scarlet had to laugh at the horrified expression on Lewis's face.

Jessie turned back to Scarlet. "He admitted he did something stupid and hurt your feelings. He's not sure if he asks you out if you'd even say yes. He says he's waiting for the right moment, but waiting is making him cranky. So would you go out with him?"

"Don't answer that," Lewis said to Scarlet. Then he turned to Jessie, "That's a conversation Scarlet and I will have in private."

"I guess that's my cue to leave. But before I go, just so we're clear," Jessie said. "Not to put pressure on the two of you or anything, but having Scarlet as my next mom would be totally awesome." She walked over to give Scarlet a hug. "If I had a say," she whispered. "You'd be my choice."

"I love you, Jess," Scarlet said, squeezing her tight. "No matter what happens between me and your dad, that will never change."

"I'm glad," Jess said. "Now," she stepped out of Scarlet's embrace. "I am going to disappear into my very own bedroom—which I love, love, love, by the way, and thank you thank you thank you for my purple wall—to let you adults talk." She walked toward her bedroom.

When she was out of sight Lewis said, "I screwed up."

Jessie called out, "He screws up a lot. But—"

"I don't need any more help," Lewis yelled to her.

"Shutting up now," Jessie called back, her words followed by the slam of her door.

"I think that's her favorite part of having a door," Lewis said.

Scarlet smiled.

After an awkward pause they both said, "I'm sorry," at the exact same time.

"You have nothing to be sorry about," Lewis quickly added.

"I was awful to you last Monday. I dumped the brunt of my anger on you and you didn't deserve it." Doing so had made her feel even worse after he'd left. And she'd spent a good part of her week trying to figure out how to apologize.

He looked at her with such concern, such caring. "You had every right to be upset. After what I did, seeing my face made you feel worse. I understand."

"But I appreciate the gesture. I really do." It'd just taken a few days.

"Come sit down." He put his hand at her low back to guide her to his black leather sofa, and Scarlet's body came alive on contact, like it always did when he touched her. She sat and he sat beside her, taking her hand in his and resting both on his thigh. "I want to tell you what I should have said Sunday morning."

"It's okay. It's over. I'd prefer to move on and not re-visit it." Since she'd finally come to terms with the fact there couldn't be more than friendship between them.

"You scare me," he said.

She looked up at him. "How nice of you to share." Since she was still a little shaky on the emotional stability front, she directed the conversation to a more neutral topic, "So did Jessie have fun in Lake George?"

Apparently Lewis would not be sidetracked. "You make me feel things and want things I've never felt or wanted before, things that before meeting you I was convinced I'd never feel or want."

Could he be any vaguer? "What kind of things?" she asked.

He stared into her eyes. "Long term things."

Scarlet wasn't sure how she felt about that.

"But I'd grown to care for you so much, so

deeply in such a short amount of time. I didn't believe it was real. How could it be? We've only known each other for a few weeks. It's not normal to think about spending the rest of your life with someone after only a few weeks. Heck, for someone like me it's unprecedented."

He brought her hand to his lips and kissed it.

"Yet there I was," he continued. "Lying in bed with you, picturing a long happy life of waking up with you by my side. But the longer I lay there, the more it seemed too good to be true, the more I convinced myself it had to be the circumstances that'd brought us together. I was grateful, and dare I admit maybe a little dependent on you for your help with Jessie. And it'd been so long since I'd been intimate with a woman."

"I'm not sure I like where this is headed," Scarlet admitted.

"My thoughts were all jumbled. Then you woke up and startled me and I have no idea why 'It's over. This can't happen again,' were the first words to fly out of my mouth but they did. Once they were out I couldn't take them back because I wasn't ready to commit to what asking you to stay would have meant."

"Then I got mad and stormed off."

"You had every right to. If I were you I'd have hit me."

Scarlet smiled. "I'll remember that for next time."

"There won't be a next time." He brought her hand up and pressed it to his heart. "What I should have told you when you woke up in my arms last Sunday morning is I see how smart and special you are. I appreciate all of your wonderful, caring qualities and I value you and your friendship more than any other woman out there."

The fact that he'd remembered her speech to sooth a broken-hearted Jessie almost word for word touched Scarlet.

"You're important to me," he said. "I want to find a way to make us work, I want us to be together, but I need time," he said. "I should have told you all that, but I didn't. So now I'm asking for another chance. If we can take it slow, I promise to do my best to piss you off as little as possible, as long as you're willing to cut me some slack here and there. I'm entering into new territory here."

"New territory?"

"Exclusivity, a committed relationship, with you."

Scarlet sat there, unsure what to say in response to his sincere words.

Lewis picked up on her uncertainty. "Unless that's not what you want…" He released her hand.

"I care about you, I really do." But she'd spent a lot of time thinking about her future lately, and she'd decided not to give up on her desire to have a baby either naturally or via adoption or IVF. "I don't think we're looking for the same things in a relationship. If I'm going to date a man exclusively, at this stage in my life, it'll be with the intention of getting married and having babies and a house with a yard where I can plant flowers. I want a big family filled with love." It's what she'd dreamed of for so long and time was running out. "If those things aren't part of your plans for the future," and she was pretty sure they weren't, "I think we're better off as friends."

"For you, I'm open to anything. Everything," Lewis said. "You're the only woman I'd consider for my bride. But how about we date for a while to make sure it's the right choice for both of us. If we decide it is, you want babies, I'll give you babies. You want a house with a yard, we'll find one. You want a big family, for you I'll accept mom's standing invitation for weekly Sunday dinner."

For the first time since losing Joey, Scarlet felt a return of hope for a happy future. "I'd like that."

"Regardless of what happens, as of today you and Jessie and I are family. When you're alone in your apartment, you'll never be completely alone because we're only a phone call away. You need company, you come here, it's getting late, you sleepover."

"I don't think that's a good idea." Not with Jessie around.

"In the loft," he said. "After you help me pick out a big comfortable futon to put up there."

So sweet. "Thank you."

He leaned in and whispered, "But after Jessie goes to bed we can…" he wiggled his eyebrows.

"I'd like that, too," she whispered back.

"So where do you want to go on our first official date as a couple?" he asked. "To seal the deal, so to speak."

Scarlet thought for a moment. "How about we take Jessie to see her first Broadway play?"

He sat back and looked at her. "You want to include Jessie on our date?"

"Of course I do," she said. "We're a family." She loved the way that sounded, the way it felt. To be part of a family. Her family. She smiled and moved in close. "But afterwards I want you all to myself."

Lewis pulled her onto his lap. "And you can have me all night long." He kissed her.

Jessie picked that moment to call out. "Are you guys almost done? Can I come out now?"

Scarlet jumped to her own spot on the couch and dried her lips on her wrist. Lewis adjusted his pants and crossed one leg over the other. "Yes," they both answered together.

"Good," Jessie said, coming back into the living room. "Because I just remembered I have a question." She walked over to the coat closet, opened the door, and pointed at the coats piled on the sleeping bag on the floor topped off by the broken metal rod. "What the heck happened in there?"

Lewis leaned in, put his hand up to shield his mouth from Jessie, and whispered, "Dating with a teenager in residence is not going to be easy."

To which Scarlet whispered back, "When something's important you find a way to make it work. And you, Lewis Jackson, are very important, to me, too."

* * * * *